"We can't. No." She shook her head and took a step back. "This doesn't solve anything."

Not everything, he mentally agreed. But in his opinion they were certainly heading down the right path. "I know it doesn't," he admitted. "But—"

"Why did you come?" she asked in a trembling voice. "Why couldn't you have stayed away?"

"Because—"

As if she'd gathered every bit of strength from within, she squared her shoulders and her eyes flashed fire. "You need to go. Out of my house. Out of my hospital. Out of our *life!*"

"I know this is tough—"

"You have no idea," she said bitterly.

"But it isn't easy for me either. I'd go if I could, but I can't, Sabrina," he said flatly. "Not after knowing we made a beautiful boy. Don't ask that of me, because I can't. I just can't."

Jessica Matthews's interest in medicine began at a young age, and she nourished it with medical stories and hospital-based television programmes. After a stint as a teenage candy-striper, she pursued a career as a clinical laboratory scientist. When not writing or on duty, she fills her day with countless family and school-related activities. Jessica lives in the central United States, with her husband, daughter and son.

Recent titles by the same author:

THE BABY DOCTOR'S BRIDE
THE ROYAL DOCTOR'S BRIDE

HIS BABY BOMBSHELL

BY
JESSICA MATTHEWS

MILLS & BOON

First published in Great Britain 2009
Large Print edition 2010
Harlequin Mills & Boon Limited,
Eton House, 18-24 Paradise Road,
Richmond, Surrey TW9 1SR

© Jessica Matthews 2009

ISBN: 978 0 263 21073 6

Harlequin Mills & Boon policy is to use papers that are
natural, renewable and recyclable products and made
from wood grown in sustainable forests. The logging and
manufacturing process conform to the legal environmental
regulations of the country of origin.

Printed and bound in Great Britain
by CPI Antony Rowe, Chippenham, Wiltshire

HIS BABY
BOMBSHELL

To my husband Terry,
my personal 'go to' guy for my golfing
questions. To my daughter Jessica, for all
those golf tournaments I was privileged to
watch you play, and to my son Matt,
for the music you bring to my life.

CHAPTER ONE

SABRINA HOLLISTER knew she'd eventually see Dr Adrian McReynolds again, but she'd never dreamed that moment would come unexpectedly at a golf course or that she'd knock him senseless in the process.

After a year of leaving her equipment in the back of her single-car garage to collect dust, her friend and fellow nurse Kate Ostmeyer had convinced her to brush off the cobwebs and participate in the First Annual Pinehaven Health Center Benefit Golf Tournament.

Although her first- and second-hole scores weren't anything to brag about, she'd parred the next few before shooting an unbelievable eagle on seven. Not bad for a woman who hadn't swung a club since early last season.

Between the excitement of continuing her game from where she'd left off and the thrill of being outdoors, instead of stuck inside on this beautiful summer day, life couldn't have been better.

Until the eighth hole.

Sabrina took her first tee-off practice swing seconds before Kate completely shattered her concentration.

"Mercy Memorial is loaning us one of their ER docs," Kate announced, clearly proud of her news scoop.

Sabrina froze and she felt her palms break out into a sweat inside her gloves. *Steady*, she cautioned herself. *Don't jump to conclusions.*

Determined to only sound mildly interested instead of frantic, she asked, "Really? They've never loaned us one before."

"There's a first time for everything," the OB nurse remarked cheerfully. "And why shouldn't Mercy send us a doctor? They're part of our consortium and the corporate folks decided that every hospital in the group would take their turn helping cover our ED until we hired a permanent physician. It's Mercy's turn."

Mercy's turn or not, Sabrina scolded herself for leaping to conclusions. The man she'd known at her former place of employment surely wouldn't be the one who would come to her new stomping ground. However, her reassurance didn't stop her from mentally crossing her fingers as she struggled to inject the right note of idle curiosity into her voice. "When is this happening? Not for a few weeks, I hope."

"Oh, he's already here. Started today. In fact, he's playing in this tournament. Apparently our chief of staff wants to make a good impression so he insisted on including him as a member of his foursome."

Sabrina didn't care what Dr Mosby wanted. She did, however, care about working with whomever Mercy had sent. As a member of the nursing float pool, Sabrina was temporarily assigned to the emergency department until one of the regularly assigned nurses returned from maternity leave. Which meant she'd be sharing space with the new guy for the next three weeks.

Don't let it be Adrian.

Sabrina gritted her teeth and asked the obvious. "Do you know who he is?"

"I forget his name," Kate admitted sheepishly. "But, hey, you worked there before you joined us, so I'm sure if you mention a few, I'll recognize his."

"I've been gone for ages," Sabrina pointed out. "Turnover was high. The ED folks I knew probably aren't there any more."

She wasn't telling a lie. Mercy always had new

ER docs coming and going, although it boasted a core group who'd remained the same over the years. If hospital administration had been asked to supply a physician, most likely the ED director would assign one of the newbies. Those with seniority wouldn't be sent to another facility without good reason or unless they'd volunteered. She couldn't imagine Adrian offering to leave his house and his job when his gesture meant he'd be an hour and a half away from his family.

Family. She was both envious that he had a family to call his own and bitter that he'd refused to share it with her. But both of those emotions were counter-productive, so she stuffed them back into the mental box where she stored "subjects not to think about".

Kate tapped a forefinger on her chin in obvious thought. "All I remember is that it started with an 'M'."

Sabrina ran through the few names she recalled, eliminating one in particular. "Monighan, Miller, Magee…"

"Close, but not quite. Mac something, I think."

Her chest tightened as only one person fit Kate's criteria. "McReynolds?"

Kate snapped her fingers. "That's right. Dr McReynolds."

Sabrina's entire world suddenly changed from living color to shades of gray. Blood rushed through her ears, drowning out all sound, and her heart seemed to thump through her chest.

Adrian was coming. No, he was already here.

Heaven help her!

She'd wanted to put off meeting him in this lifetime until she was mentally and emotionally prepared to face him again—preferably in about fifteen or twenty years. Clearly, she'd have minutes or at most twenty-four hours, which wasn't nearly long enough for her to develop any sort of game plan.

She'd dated Adrian for about six months and by the end of that time their relationship had subtly shifted to the point where they'd discussed theoretical topics such as how many children they'd like to have, the sort of house they'd want to live in, which area of Denver had the best elementary schools. They'd been on the verge of a commitment, she believed, when everything changed in an instant.

While riding his motorcycle, Adrian's twenty-four-year-old brother Clay had been sideswiped by a minivan on Interstate 70. He'd come into the ER more broken than whole, with his prognosis of being a paraplegic if his broken vertebrae had damaged his spinal column. Only time would tell.

Determined to help the man she loved to bear the burden of caring for Clay, she'd been crushed when Adrian had broken off their relationship because "he had to focus completely on his brother". Although she'd tried to convince him that she wasn't asking him to put her ahead of his brother's needs, each passing day and failed attempt to see him had caused her hopes and dreams to slowly die. Finally, she'd surrendered to the inevitable and gave up trying to talk to him. Determined to avoid reminders of the man she'd grown to love and the places where they'd spent happy hours, she'd resigned her position at Mercy Memorial and headed for the growing northeastern suburb of Pinehaven, where she'd moved on with her life, just as Adrian had wanted.

Now he had the audacity to appear and upset her hard-won composure. Yet she couldn't deny the hope that suddenly blossomed in her chest. Could he have volunteered because she was here and he wanted to see her? After all, as an ED physician with seniority, he normally wouldn't have been chosen for an assignment like this.

But as the possibility raised her spirits, she warned herself to be cautious. Better for her to keep her imagination under control and not jump to conclusions. Extremely high hopes had a tendency to fall hard and land more painfully.

When she really thought about his arrival logically, it didn't make sense for Adrian to tie himself to a job for three months just to see her again when he could have found her quite easily by other means. She may not have specifically given him her new address, but she hadn't moved to Pinehaven in secret—any number of her ex-coworkers knew her destination. If he'd wanted to talk to her, he would have telephoned, emailed, or appeared on her front porch before now, especially if one considered how Pinehaven Health Center wasn't far from Mercy—a mere ninety minutes' drive if traffic was heavy, less if it wasn't. No, if Adrian had truly and temporarily relocated here, he'd only come under duress.

The realization hardened her heart.

"Do you know him?" Kate asked, curiosity coloring her face.

Did she know Adrian McReynolds? What a question!

She knew details. He liked his coffee black, his food spicy, his work and living spaces clean and neat. He wore boxer shorts to bed, had silky smooth hair on his chest, developed five o'clock shadow twice a day, had the faintest scar near his left temple's hairline and a birthmark on his right hip, and was a fantastic lover. He was charming, had a wonderful sense of humor, was devoted to his younger siblings, and locked away his deepest feelings behind a wall of stoicism that only a few could breach.

On the job, he was a perfectionist and demanded the best for his patients. He was completely im-movable once he'd made a decision. At one time, she'd admired the trait because it showed tenacity, persistence and strength of character. Now she only saw it as a flaw of closed-mindedness.

Did she know Adrian McReynolds? Apparently not as well as she should have or as well as she'd once thought.

She hesitated before answering. Until she consid-ered the ramifications of what his presence would do to her life, she refused to admit anything but the barest of details. She didn't want people to know they'd once been quite close or that he'd ended the relationship because he didn't want to make room in his life for her, so she stretched the truth almost to the breaking point.

"I've run into him a few times," she said instead.

"Then I'm sure he'll appreciate seeing a familiar

face now that he's here for the next few months. And speaking of faces, the stranger over there with Dr Mosby's team must be our fellow."

Sabrina lowered her club to study the group approaching the thirteenth green about fifty yards to her right. Instinctively, her gaze homed on the tall individual she hadn't seen in thirteen months, one week and two days.

Even from this distance, she recognized his confident bearing, his long-legged walk, and his lucky black-and-purple Colorado Rockies baseball cap.

It was Adrian. The man she'd never expected to see until she'd plotted out every second of their next encounter, until she could think of him as a casual acquaintance rather than a lover, until she could face him with the cool indifference he deserved.

As aloof as she wanted to be, as often as she'd told herself she'd relegated him into her past and moved on with her life, seeing him with hardly any advance warning brought all of those painful emotions to the surface.

Her chest hurt as she realized his presence affected more than her own heart. His untimely arrival complicated everything she'd built for herself during the past year. She'd prided herself on her ability to work with anyone and everyone, but working with Adrian on a daily basis for several weeks was a punishment she didn't deserve.

If disrupting her professional life wasn't enough, he'd turn her personal life into a shambles, too. Pinehaven might be a suburb of Denver, but the people in this community were a close-knit group. Secrets were impossible to keep. All he had to do was ask the right question, and well-meaning people would share her meticulously vague story.

The same story to which only he could piece together all the bitter details.

Thank goodness his name had never crossed her lips. No one would associate him with the fellow who'd dumped her, not even Kate, her best friend and the OB nurse who'd coached her through her labor.

Tears of frustration blurred her vision and she rapidly blinked them away, hating the inevitability of Adrian turning her world into chaos after she'd finally, and with extreme effort, whipped it in order.

Instantly, her lungs seemed to deflate and she ran through the full gamut of emotions before finally settling on panic.

"Are we going to play or stand here all day?" Molly Blake, a third member of their Rusty Clubs foursome, whined as she swiped her forehead. "You guys might prefer to swelter under the sun, but I'd rather hang out in the air-conditioned clubhouse."

Sabrina's flight-or-fight response kicked into high gear. The only thought running through her mind was to escape before Adrian saw her. Contrary to what Kate might believe about familiar faces, Sabrina needed to postpone their imminent reunion so she could mentally prepare herself.

Numb, Sabrina stepped up to her ball and swung blindly. As soon as her driver made contact, she knew without even looking that she'd sliced the ball.

Time slowed as she watched it head in Adrian's direction like a computer-guided missile searching for its target. Oh, surely fate wouldn't be that cruel!

"Fore," she yelled just before the projectile struck her nemesis on the side of his head.

He dropped like a rock and lay motionless on the manicured grass.

Horrified, Sabrina's club slipped from her hand as her heart pounded. Dear God, she'd killed him!

She'd killed the father of her son.

"What the—?" Adrian squinted up at the blue sky, seeing stars when none had been a few moments ago. His head throbbed in time to his heartbeat and something warm trickled down his ear and neck.

"Just lie still for a few minutes, son." A worried face hovered over his, blocking the sun from his eyes. "Give yourself a chance to recover."

The world spun at all sorts of crazy angles, so he gratefully complied. "What happened?"

"Golf ball." Mosby pressed a semi-clean golf towel to a spot above Adrian's left ear. "How's the head?"

He took stock. "Sore."

"Any dizziness, nausea?"

"Some," he admitted, hoping the power of positive thinking would slow down the spinning and churning of his internal amusement park ride from Tilt-A-Whirl to a sedate carousel.

Mosby peered into his eyes. "Pupils are equal and reactive, so you can rest easy on that account."

"I'm OK. Just give me…a minute."

"Take all the time you need," Mosby advised, placing a hand on his shoulder. "An ambulance is on its way."

"Not necessary," he croaked, hating to appear weak, especially on his first official day in town. "I'm supposed to *work* in ER, not check in as a patient."

"It's very necessary," Mosby assured him. "We take care of our own, and as of eight o'clock this morning, you're one of us."

Adrian folded one arm over his eyes, too befuddled to argue and quite content to lie on the grass until his wits returned. He heard voices and tried to focus on them through the pounding in his head, but none seemed to make any sense until he heard one so familiar it haunted him in his dreams.

"How is he? Is he OK? He's breathing, isn't he?" *Sabrina.*

He'd known he'd see her again—the hospital wasn't large enough to avoid it—but he wondered if her breathless concern would fade as soon as she realized that *he* was the one lying on the ground with a goose egg on the side of his head.

He lowered his arm and opened his eyes to see her face above his. Through his slightly blurry vision, he recognized her retroussé nose, high cheekbones, kissable mouth and eyes as black as midnight. "Yeah, I'm breathing and talking," he answered for himself. "In a few minutes I'll be walking, too."

"That was one helluva slice," Mosby commented. "I wonder who hit it?"

Even with his head feeling as if his brains had been run through a blender, Adrian was alert enough to watch color wash over Sabrina's face. "I did," she admitted.

Of all the people in this tournament, Sabrina had

knocked him senseless? He wanted to laugh at the irony but his skull hurt too much. The best he could do was smile, and that turned out to be more grimace than grin.

As he covered his eyes with his arm once again to wait for the paramedics, one thought ran through his mind as clearly as a church bell on a calm summer day.

Paybacks were hell.

After seeing Adrian awake and alert, Sabrina felt marginally better, until she saw his ashen face and the blood trickling past his ear and down his corded neck to stain his shirt collar. In spite of everything that had gone wrong between them, in spite of past hurts, she'd never dreamed of physically harming him. Not that he didn't deserve it, of course…

"I'm so sorry," she murmured. "It was an accident. Honest."

"Of course it was," Mosby declared. "No one deliberately slices the ball."

"That's right," she concurred, hoping Adrian wouldn't accuse her of evil intent, at least not in front of this crowd of witnesses. "If it's any consolation, I've never hit anyone before."

"Or you haven't been told," Adrian remarked

dryly. "That would have been quite a drive if it had gone straight."

"Probably," she agreed.

An ambulance siren wailed in the distance and he visibly winced, then sighed. "For me, I suppose."

"Afraid so," Mosby said.

"What if I don't want it?"

Sabrina ignored his petulant tone. He'd hated receiving attention and today's incident would forever mark him in the hospital staff's collective minds. As a man who preferred to remain out of the limelight, he'd never forgive her for the notoriety.

Then again, he had worse things to hold against her than being the subject of well-meant gossip. Never telling him about their son topped this incident by a country mile. Oh, he'd no doubt be furious, but she'd endured too much during and after her pregnancy with no one but herself to rely upon to be afraid of his reaction. She'd had her reasons and as far as she was concerned they had been the right ones, but her bravado didn't stop her from checking his hand for a wedding ring.

No ring. Not even a pale tan line marked his third finger.

How curious, especially after what she'd seen…

"Sorry, young man, but when you go back to

Mercy, you'll go none the worse for wear," Mosby replied. "If everything checks out, you can report for work in the morning."

Either Adrian recognized the finality in Dr Mosby's voice or he'd realized that an ambulance ride wasn't such a bad idea because he didn't argue.

"Sabrina?" Mosby turned his attention to her. "Follow Adrian to the hospital and make sure he's given VIP treatment. Nothing's too good for our newest physician."

Oh, sweet baby Jane. "Me?" she protested, before she realized that refusing would only foster unwanted speculation.

Mosby studied her. "Why not you?"

Why not her, indeed? She could give him a specific reason—Adrian had told her that he didn't want her in his life—but mentioning their volatile past wasn't appropriate under the circumstances. Fortunately, the perfect excuse popped into her head.

"I'm not sure he'd appreciate me doing the honors when I'm the one responsible for his condition." She glanced helplessly at Adrian, hoping, *expecting* him to refuse her company.

"Nonsense," Mosby declared. "Dr McReynolds is a professional as well as a golfer. Accidents happen. He won't hold this against you."

She wasn't as certain, but she bit back a reply because anything she could have said would have raised questions she didn't want to answer.

"I suspect you won't play worth a hoot after this anyway, so your team will probably thank me." The chief of staff added with a twinkle in his eye, "It may also be safer for the masses if you aren't swinging a club."

Great. She'd never live this incident down, either. For a woman who'd won regional tournaments in both high school and college, she'd rather be known for a brilliant achievement instead of a hapless slice that had knocked out a fellow golfer and sent him to hospital.

Mosby laid a hand on Adrian's shoulder. "Never fear. We won't abandon you. Will we, Sabrina?" he asked with a pointed glance in her direction.

She glanced at Adrian, wondering why he consented to Mosby's plans. While he truly wasn't in a position to refuse any more than she could, she wondered if he was simply too confused to realize what was happening. Accident or not, she felt guilty for causing his injury.

"I'll get my things," she said reluctantly, hoping she wouldn't be forced to contact his sisters with bad news. Conditions such as skull fractures, subdural hematomas and nerve damage were serious possibilities. Although it was a shame he hadn't shown initial signs of amnesia. It would solve a lot of her problems, she thought wryly.

"Good. I'll check in with you as soon as we've finished our round. We'll have test results by then."

"Paramedics are here," someone said, and the small crowd parted.

Sabrina stood off to one side, watching the emergency personnel apply a cervical collar and prepare Adrian for transport. The grim set to his mouth and his one-word replies suggested his head hurt worse than he cared to admit. Surprisingly enough, his vulnerability tugged at her heartstrings.

You'd feel the same for any injured person, she told herself, refusing to believe she held any tender feelings for him at all. After the way he'd treated her, thrown her love away like yesterday's garbage, how pitiful would she be if she did? In another lifetime, she would have been more than happy to escort him to the hospital and act as his hospital liaison, but too much had happened since those blissful days. Far better for her peace of mind if she treated him warily or, at best, as a familiar stranger until she discovered why he'd taken this temporary position at Pinehaven Health Center.

An uneasy thought came to her. Did he know about Jeremy?

No, she decided. She hadn't mentioned her pregnancy to anyone before she'd left Denver. Since then she hadn't run into any of her old friends and her new ones had never heard Adrian McReynolds' name until today. For the moment, her secret was safe, although she'd have to deal with it sooner than she'd anticipated.

She caught a ride back to the parking lot in a tournament official's golf cart, loaded her clubs, then followed the ambulance to the hospital.

By the time the paramedics had unloaded Adrian and installed him in a trauma room, he sported an IV in his hand, a pulse oximeter on his finger, and a long-suffering expression on his handsome face.

The old Sabrina would have teased out a smile because she hated to see him ill at ease, but the new Sabrina refused to let herself feel anything but objective concern. As far as she and the rest of the world were concerned, he was just another patient, even if he could legally use the initials "MD" behind his name.

"Would you like me to call anyone for you?" she asked politely after the ER doctor had examined him and they were waiting for the lab and radiology staff to arrive. "Your wife? Girlfriend? Or a family member?"

"No." His blue-gray gaze met hers. "Don't call a single soul."

"I'm sure someone would want to know what's happened."

"There isn't anything to tell to anyone," he said shortly. "This is a minor injury and not worth the trouble it would cause."

So much for finding out if he'd ever replaced her... "Suit yourself, but if you should change your mind, let me know."

"I won't."

"As stubborn as ever, I see," she remarked, already breaking her first rule to treat him as a stranger she'd met a few minutes earlier.

"I just want to play the hospital's game so I can go back to my apartment where I can recuperate on my own."

Knowing Mosby as she did, Adrian wouldn't be heading back to his apartment as quickly as he thought, but someone else could break the news. On the other hand, Adrian hated not being in control, so if she planted the idea, maybe he'd resign himself to his fate before he got official word from The Man himself. Why she wanted to prepare him for the eventuality, she didn't know, other than dealing with his surliness ranked at the bottom of her list of things she wanted to do.

There was a silver lining, though. She hadn't wanted to be Adrian's guardian angel in the first place, so if he gave her the slightest bit of trouble, she'd shovel it right back, in spades.

In fact, now that she thought about the situation, he wouldn't have to complain too much for her to do so.

"Dr Mosby may decide to keep you overnight," she mentioned offhandedly, testing his reaction.

He frowned. "Why? You don't admit every person in the hospital for a bump on the head."

"No, but you aren't just any person." She ticked off the reasons on the fingers of her left hand. "One, you're a doctor, which means you get special consideration. Two, Mosby is determined to treat you like spun gold, not only because he wants to impress you but because he wants you to speak fondly of us when you go back home."

"Ah. For recruitment purposes, I presume."

"Probably," she agreed. "This position has been vacant for some time so I'm sure he intends to take advantage of whatever opportunities he can to show us in a good light. The question for the moment though is, who would monitor you through the night if Dr Mosby discharges you? Unless, of course, you aren't staying alone." She raised an eyebrow.

"Fishing, Sabrina?"

"Not at all," she said, airily indifferent, although deep down she wanted to know if he had allowed a significant other into his life. Not that she cared one way or another, of course. She was only being curious.

"Your living arrangements don't concern me. However, they could factor into Mosby's decision, so I thought you might appreciate the advance warning. If not, pretend I didn't say a word."

He fell silent as if mulling over his situation. "I don't suppose the crickets count as companions?"

"Not unless they can take your vital signs and call 911 if necessary."

"I was afraid you'd say that." He sighed. "Then, yes, I'm all by myself."

"I'm surprised." She hadn't realized she'd spoken aloud until he answered.

"Why would you think that?"

She evaded the question. "I assumed you would have brought Clay with you." After Clay's discharge from hospital, Adrian had moved him into his own home to oversee and assist in his rehabilitation.

"He's living by himself these days."

Relief at the news made her forget to treat Adrian with cool disdain. "Oh, Adrian, I'm so glad. Then he's all right? I've wondered and worried about him…" Realizing she'd said too much, she cut herself off. When Adrian had severed their ties, he'd also severed her relationship to his family members and she missed them almost as much as she'd missed Adrian. Oh, she could have kept in touch with Clay, but it would have been an awkward situation for both of them, so she hadn't.

"He hasn't completely recovered," he admitted. "It took awhile before he could start therapy and then his progress came slowly, but he's graduated from a walker to a cane, which was quite a cause for celebration."

"I can imagine." And she could. She pictured Adrian, Clay, Marcy and Susan barbecuing in Adrian's back yard. Adrian liked to wear his "Kiss the Cook" apron and chef's hat and monitor the status of his burgers with the same intensity as an anesthesiologist monitoring a surgical patient. Clay had often stolen the green olives out from under Marcy's watchful eye while Susan had scolded him for spoiling his dinner. Adrian's portable CD player had usually provided the ambience while Sabrina had acted as the official and unbiased taste tester of Marcy's culinary concoctions.

She wondered who did the honors now, then jerked herself off that fruitless and painful path. The McReynolds family wasn't part of her life and never would be. For her own peace of mind, she had to remember that.

"In any case…" She steered the conversation back to the original topic. "If you're living alone, I'd plan to spend the night in a luxurious private suite on our spacious second floor."

"If it's a matter of having a babysitter, you could do the honors," he said in a clearly hopeful tone.

Coming from anyone else, she would have laughed and countered with a saucy answer, but the offer came from Adrian, which made his suggestion no laughing matter. If he didn't look so pathetic, she'd tell him exactly what she thought of his idea, using words capable of blistering the walls' semi-gloss enamel paint.

But he *did* look rather forlorn and pitiful and she let her opportunity slide. There would be plenty of others when she could fully vent her anger and not feel lower than pond scum for verbally attacking a concussed man. A confrontation was inevitable.

"Sorry, but I don't do private nursing. And even if I did, I have laundry waiting at home."

"You wouldn't have to stay," he coaxed. "Just long enough so Mosby thinks I'm not alone."

She eyed him carefully and forced herself not to succumb to his pleading, puppy-dog-in-the-window expression. "I won't put myself in the position where you can tell the chief of staff I ran out on you halfway through the night."

"I wouldn't."

He must think her to be a complete fool if she'd trust him the minute she'd laid eyes on him, and she was not a fool. "Sorry, but that's the sort of favor I'd only do for a friend."

"We were friends once."

"We were," she conceded, "but not any more. Considering our past, aren't you afraid I'll slip arsenic into your coffee or smother you in your sleep?"

"I'll take the chance, Bree," he said dryly, "because we both know I won't get any rest here. And…" He paused. "I'd hoped we could…talk."

So Adrian wanted to talk, did he? She'd suffered through too many hurts to think that a simple heart-to-heart at this late date would clear the air and heal old wounds. He'd betrayed her trust and she couldn't imagine any way he would possibly earn it again.

"You aren't in any condition to carry on a conversation," she said calmly, grateful for her ready-made excuse because the thought of discussing anything more serious than a weather forecast released a flock of butterflies in her stomach. The day for an in-depth conversation would come, but only when she was ready.

"Maybe not at this moment, but—"

"I'm not interested in rehashing ancient history," she warned. "Not now. Not ever."

"A year isn't ancient history."

"It is to me." That year was a lifetime ago—Jeremy's lifetime. Events before then weren't worth the time or energy to dwell upon.

"Sabrina—" he began.

The curtain swooshed and a young man carrying a phlebotomy tray walked in. "Oh, my," she said in a too-bright tone that hinted at her eagerness for the interruption, "Lab's here. It's Dracula time."

Seizing the opportunity to gain much-needed breathing space, she walked out of the trauma room while the technician drew Adrian's blood samples. Unfortunately, physical distance didn't settle her thoughts, as she'd hoped.

Wishing she hadn't sliced the ball like a novice and landed in her present position, Sabrina idled away the hours while he was poked, prodded, and CT-scanned. From time to time, like any good nurse, she exchanged his magazines from the waiting room's well-thumbed collection, brought ice chips when he complained about being thirsty, and covered him with a warm blanket when she found him huddled under the sheet, half-asleep. Although she'd like to leave him to his own devices, Dr Mosby would ask Adrian about the care and personal attention he'd received, so she simply gritted her teeth and treated her nemesis as if he truly were a VIP.

Although, she decided with wicked glee, in his case the "I" stood for "irritating" rather than "important."

Through it all, and somewhat to her surprise because Adrian didn't accept defeat easily, he dropped the subject and stared impatiently at the clock. His gloomy mood didn't improve until Dr Beth Iverson returned with his results.

"Do you want me to stay or leave you two alone?" Sabrina asked before the doctor could share anything that Adrian might consider a violation of his privacy.

"You may as well hear the verdict for yourself," he grudgingly offered. "Go ahead, Doctor. Tell me what I already know—I'm fine. No cracks, no nerve damage, nothing!"

"At the risk of making your head swell more than it has," Beth said cheerfully, "you're right. Lab work looks great and no skull fractures or hematomas appeared on the scan. Your cut bled a lot and you can get by without stitches, although I'd like to put in a few to prevent the edges from separating too easily."

Adrian looked quite smug as he met Sabrina's gaze. "What did I tell you? I have a hard head."

In more ways than one, Sabrina silently agreed.

Beth continued. "You'll probably have a headache and some nausea for awhile—concussions will do that, you know, and as yours is mild, those symptoms shouldn't last long. Continue with the ice packs and acetaminophen for the pain."

"Will do. Now, if someone will give me my clothes, I'm going to my home away from home."

Beth shook her head, her eyes apologetic. "Sorry. John wants to keep you overnight. As a precaution."

"You don't need someone as healthy as I am taking up bed space," he coaxed in the charming manner that allowed him to get his own way more often than not.

Beth smiled. "I have my orders. There's a bed upstairs with your name on it."

His smile turned into a frown. "This is so unnecessary," he groused.

"Take it up with the boss," the doctor advised. "I'm just the hired help. After I stitch up your head, Sabrina will see you're settled in your room. If you need anything, call me. I'm on duty until seven."

She quickly closed the gash with neat sutures. After pronouncing her work finished, she breezed out of the room and left Sabrina to deal with an unhappy Adrian.

"Wheelchair or gurney for the next leg of your trip?" she asked, relieved to know her golf ball hadn't done lasting damage. She wouldn't admit it either, but she was privately glad he'd be under close observation for awhile. Problems weren't always detected immediately and could develop over time. It would be far better for him, and for her peace of mind, to spend his first night in Pinehaven under a nurse's watchful eye.

"I'll walk."

She shook her head. "Not on my watch, buster. Physician or not, you're a patient, which means I'm in charge for the moment. Nor will I let it be said that I don't abide by the rules. So what'll it be? A wheelchair or a gurney?"

He glared. "Wheelchair."

"Then sit tight and I'll be right back."

Transferring him to the medical floor went smoothly and silently, which came as a relief. She wasn't in the mood for small talk and clearly he wasn't either. However, once she'd braked his wheelchair and pointed to the hospital gown on the edge of the bed, he shook his head and crossed his arms.

"I may have to stay here unnecessarily, but I'll do it in my own clothes," he stated regally.

"And how do you propose they get here?"

He raised an eyebrow. "Need you ask?"

She held up her hands to object, but he didn't give her the opportunity.

"You landed me in these spacious accommodations with your wicked slice," he reminded her. "In my books, that's a debt you have to pay."

"If every other patient can wear the stylish apparel we so thoughtfully provide, so can you. And if you're worried about your hiney showing, stay in bed."

"*Hiney?* My, my," he said dryly, "your professional vocabulary is amazing."

"That's what continuing education is for."

"Whatever you call my hiney, buns, or posterior, there's the matter of you being responsible for my VIP care. As a VIP, I want my own shorts and

T-shirt, not a flimsy, see-through, doesn't-close-in-the-back hospital gown."

No question about it—the "I" definitely meant irritating.

"But you don't sleep in anything except your boxers," she blurted out.

"At home, I don't. Does this…" he waved his arms in an all-encompassing motion "…even remotely look like home?"

Sensing the futility in arguing—apparently he'd decided that if cajolery wouldn't get what he wanted, arrogance and his rank would—she heaved a sigh. "OK, fine. I presume you also want a change of clothes for tomorrow and your toothbrush?"

"Yeah. Don't forget my electric razor either." He dug in his trouser pocket and tossed a keyring at her before he sank gingerly into the bed. "Thanks. I'd be grateful if you'd bring them within the hour."

She caught it in mid-air, irritated by his demand. She couldn't possibly meet his hour deadline even if she'd wanted to because she was due to pick up Jeremy from the hospital's day care. Chafing under his order, she chose not to warn him she'd be late. Better to ask forgiveness after the fact than to beg permission beforehand.

"I'd also like a pizza," he informed her.

"Our cafeteria has good food. The patients all agree."

He eyed her loftily. "If I can't sleep in a real bed, then I want to eat real food. Sausage, Canadian bacon and mushrooms."

She ground her teeth. "Pizza it is. Anything else for our most illustrious personage?"

With that detail apparently settled to his satisfaction and apparently not put off by her disrespect, he closed his eyes. "No, but if I think of something, I'll call you. You do still have a cellphone?"

"Yes, I do. Who doesn't these days?"

"I'd like the number, please."

She didn't want to give it to him, but she really didn't have a choice. A notepad wasn't in sight and she didn't have a pen, so she recited the seven digits from memory.

He listened intently before satisfaction showed on his face. "Same as before."

His comment caught her off-guard. "I'm surprised you remember."

"I remember a lot of things."

"I'm happy for you," she said tartly, but a new set of questions suddenly popped into her head. If he'd wanted her out of his life so badly, why had he remembered her number? Knowing that he'd never acted on the information at his fingertips only made the intervening months of silence more painful to think about.

The sudden pressure in her chest demanded she escape before he saw this new hurt he'd caused without even trying. Immediately, she pivoted on one foot and headed for the door.

"Sabrina?" he called.

Reluctantly, she paused. "Yeah?" Sounding hoarse, she hoped he'd attribute it to grumpiness.

"For what it's worth, it's good to see you again."

She'd spent the last year shoring up her defenses against his anger and rejection, but had built nothing to protect herself against unexpected kindness. Not trusting herself to speak over the sudden lump in her throat, she simply fled.

CHAPTER TWO

"YOUR father isn't playing fair," Sabrina railed aloud as she drove to Adrian's home-away-from-home while Jeremy fussed in his car seat. "After being such a jerk, he has no right to suddenly act like a decent human being."

Jeremy chewed on his little fist and grunted as he kicked his legs and squirmed.

"I don't know what he's up to, but I'm not falling for it," she mumbled as she parked in front of the apartment complex next to Adrian's recognizable black Toyota Avalon. Apparently John Mosby had served as Adrian's taxi service and given him a ride to the golf course. "I don't care if he had a change of heart. It's too late. Too late, I tell you.

"And frankly," she continued her rant, "I'm glad my ball hit him on the head. He deserves some pain and suffering for everything he's put me through!"

Buoyed by her thoughts, she lifted Jeremy out of

his car seat, hoisted him on one hip, and headed up the sidewalk. "Come on, little man. Let's get this nasty old errand done so we can go home and play."

Carefully, she inserted the key and stepped inside.

The place reminded her of a hotel room, but Adrian had only arrived that weekend. He hadn't had time to stamp his presence on the hospital's apartment. Certain she'd find personal articles in the bathroom, she headed there first.

His toiletries lay on the counter, but she hardly noticed because the familiar scent of his favorite brand of soap hung in the air.

"What do you want for your birthday?" she asked as she cuddled against him on her sofa. "It's coming up, you know."

"I have everything I need right here." Adrian nuzzled her neck.

She giggled as he focused on a particularly ticklish spot. "I'm serious. There has to be something you'd like or need."

"Soap. Bath soap, in particular."

Sabrina pulled away to study his face. "You're kidding, aren't you?"

He shook his head. "Nope. My sisters usually shop for me and they're always buying the girly, flowery-smelling stuff."

"Ask them to choose a different scent."

"And hurt their feelings when they're trying so hard to be helpful?" He sounded horrified. *"No can do. But if someone should happen to give me a case or two and I rave about how good it smells, they'll get the hint."*

"You're quite a mastermind, aren't you?" she teased.

"I raised a younger brother and two sisters," he said matter-of-factly. *"It was the only way I could stay one step ahead of them."*

And so Sabrina had bought a dozen bars of sandalwood-scented soap which, surprisingly enough, he still used. After he'd dismissed her from his life, she would have expected him to toss out all reminders of her, including the soap, but perhaps he'd forgotten she'd gotten him hooked on it in the first place.

Idly, she grabbed his razor and his toothbrush and headed toward the bedroom. As Jeremy reached for the things in her hand and grunted his give-me noise, she allowed him to clutch the fluorescent blue toothbrush in his fierce, baby grip.

Adrian's suitcase lay open on the queen-sized bed, still containing the clothing he hadn't taken time to unpack. As she rummaged through the contents one-handed in search of underwear, socks, and the athletic apparel he'd requested, it was as if his fragrance had followed her, evoking more bitter-sweet memories—memories of soaping his back in the tub because he'd won their round of golf, celebrating her pay raise with champagne and strawberries, watching TV in his bed while feeding each other popcorn.

"You can't go back," she scolded herself. "You've moved forward, remember?"

Pushing those memories aside along with the pile of clothes she planned to deliver, she grabbed a pair of dress slacks and a short-sleeved pale green shirt from the closet, as well as his highly polished dress shoes.

He'd always polished them while he watched the evening news, she recalled, just as his father had taught him and just as he'd taught his brother Clay.

The question was, who would teach *his* son?

She glanced down at the bouncing twenty-pound joy of her life. "Sorry, kid, but spit-shining shoes wasn't part of my education. It'll be sneakers for us."

He waved the toothbrush and chortled, scraping her face with the brush end before accidentally running it through his hair like a comb.

"Be careful with that, young man," she said,

smoothing down the light brown wisps on his scalp as he stuck the smooth end into his mouth.

She placed him on the floor with his temporary toy and her set of keys while she went in search of a bag to hold Adrian's clothes. Coming up empty, she returned to the bedroom, dumped the rest of his clothes on the bed and refilled the suitcase with the things she'd selected. But when she took Adrian's toothbrush away from Jeremy, he screamed. She closed her ears to his vocal protests until she noticed several distinct tooth marks on the handle.

Great. As observant as Adrian was, he'd see the ridges and wonder how they'd gotten there. Unable to dream up a plausible explanation—it was too bad he didn't own a dog she could blame for the marks—she simply had to purchase a new one, even if it meant fighting the crowds at a store with a baby who didn't handle shopping trips very well.

By the time she had loaded Adrian's suitcase and her son into the car, Jeremy was yelling for his dinner. Adrian's specified hour was nearly over, but he'd have to wait a bit longer, she decided grimly. Jeremy's needs were more important than Adrian's comforts.

Two hours later, after dinner and an unscheduled bath to wash the strained peas out of Jeremy's hair and after she'd ordered Adrian's pizza and ran into a drug store to select a bright purple toothbrush from the hundreds on display, she pulled into the hospital parking lot. With any luck, Adrian had either slept the entire time or had gotten so engrossed in television that he hadn't noticed she was late. If he had, though, too bad. Impressing him with her efficiency and dancing to his tune weren't on her list of things to do.

Balancing a well-fed and now-happy Jeremy on her hip, she went inside.

Sabrina was late. By nearly two hours. Adrian had dozed off and on during the three hours she'd been gone, but with all the staff fluttering around him, checking his vitals, quizzing him on what day it was, did he know his birth date, how his headache and nausea was, he hadn't been able to rest for more than fifteen minutes at a time.

He grumbled aloud at how he could look forward to this well-meant but unwanted solicitous care for the remainder of the night as he pressed an ice pack to his head. The situation was enough to make a congenial man grumpy, and for the past several months he hadn't been known for his congeniality.

Oh, he may as well be honest. His good humor

had disappeared about the time he'd driven Sabrina away a year ago. Most people had attributed his curtness to his concern over Clay, but as time had marched on and Clay's condition had improved, Adrian's mood had not. In fact, it had worsened.

His siblings had compared their amateur psychology notes and had decided he needed a woman in his life to smooth his rough edges. However, after one date, he'd realized he'd spent the entire evening quietly comparing her to Sabrina. He'd suspected the poor girl had known it, too. Because no other female had interested him, his dating days had ended as abruptly as they'd begun.

Their next theory was that subconsciously he was expressing his latent anger and frustration over his broken relationship with Sabrina. That he was still mourning his loss and taking out his emotional distress on his hapless colleagues and staff members. Their answer? To get him back together with Sabrina.

Naturally, he disagreed. He was simply working too hard and doing too much. As for the ER staff, the skills of the people being hired simply weren't up to the hospital's formerly high standards.

As for his relationship with Sabrina, he believed he'd taken the high moral ground by ending it when he had. Clay needed his attention and he didn't feel it was fair to expect Sabrina to put her life on hold or be relegated to the fringes of whatever life he was free to give her. For all he knew, Clay would never leave his wheelchair and would require years of intensive therapy and personal attention from experts as well as his family.

Fortunately, his fears never panned out. While he was glad Clay's health problems hadn't turned into the worst-case scenario, as his doctors had warned, Adrian couldn't undo the past. He simply had to console himself with the knowledge that he'd made the best decision based on the information he had at the time and live with the consequences.

For him, those consequences turned him from being 'that nice Dr McReynolds' to a physician who caught nurses drawing straws in the employee lounge to see who would work with him. Even Clay's slow but steady recovery didn't improved his mood. Only one thing would—apologizing to Sabrina—but pride wouldn't allow him to take that step. What was done was done. End of story.

But it wasn't the end because his boss intervened.

"We've cut you enough slack, Adrian," Carter had told him bluntly on Friday afternoon. "I've talked to you about your attitude and you've attended several human resource seminars on inter-

personal relationships, but nothing seems to be working. I don't know why you can't pull yourself together, but I'm giving you your last chance."

"Which is?"

"Our sister hospital in Pinehaven needs a temporary ER physician and we've been asked to provide one. I'm sending you."

"Pinehaven?" The name of the town caught him by surprise and Adrian shook his head. *"I can't go there."*

Carter crossed his arms. His jaw was squared as he narrowed his eyes to study him. "Why not?"

"Because…" He drew a bracing breath. *"Because my ex-girlfriend works there. Our parting didn't…go well."* What an understatement! He'd been rude and obnoxious to make his point and he wouldn't be surprised if she threw a bedpan at him.

At first Carter didn't reply. Then he straightened in his chair and fixed his gaze on Adrian's. "Then this will be a good time for you to work out your differences, won't it?"

He initially balked at the Pinehaven assignment, but then he realized it was exactly what he needed. First, he'd swallow his pride and apologize for his former rudeness and salvage enough of their relationship so they could work in the same facility without coming to blows. Maybe, if all went well and the fates were kind, they would at least become the friends they had once been instead of remaining the bitter enemies they were now.

Secondly, as soon as he saw proof that her life was every bit as wonderful as she deserved it to be, he could finally rest knowing that he'd made the right decision. His worries and wondering would be over and he could return to Mercy Memorial emotionally whole, no longer venting his frustration on the people around him.

So far, his plan was stuck at square one. For supposedly being his liaison, she avoided him as much as possible and when she couldn't, she talked to him as eagerly as she'd participate in a rattlesnake round-up! As much as he hated having this bump on his head, his injury had paved the way for Sabrina to be his captive audience this evening. Courtesy of a talkative nurse, he'd learned Sabrina was scheduled to cover the ED this next month, which made negotiating a truce even more critical for both their sakes. Sabrina's, because she hated being a subject on the hospital grapevine and his, because if he went back to Mercy Memorial in disgrace, he'd be hunting for a new job.

Impatient and bored, he glanced at the clock once

again as he tossed the ice pack onto the bedside table. Just when he began to worry about her being delayed by something horrible like a car accident, she rushed in.

"Sorry I'm late," she said, hoisting his suitcase onto a chair. "The last few hours have been absolutely crazy."

He eyed her carefully, relieved to see her. Her shoulder-length dark brown hair was tousled, as if someone had run his hands through those soft tresses and she hadn't taken time to find a comb. She still wore the same yellow Bermuda shorts and polo shirt he'd seen earlier. And her face looked strained, as if she'd been running at full speed all day. Or, at least, since he'd seen her last.

For an instant, he felt guilty for asking her to fetch his personal things, but if he wanted to establish their personal ceasefire, he had to take advantage of whatever opportunities came his way.

Heaven help him, but after regaining his wits and seeing the wariness in her eyes, as if she expected him to act as boorishly as he had before, he *wanted* to redeem himself.

"I wish I could say the same," he remarked. "The only crazy thing I can claim is being stuck in this hospital bed for no good reason."

"How's the head?"

He didn't want to discuss his aches and pains. "Getting better as we speak," he prevaricated. "Did you have any trouble finding my stuff?"

"No, but I had a slight problem with your toothbrush and had to buy another. It's the same brand as the one you had, just a different color."

He raised an eyebrow, unable to imagine anyone having a problem with a toothbrush. It wasn't a normally breakable item. "What happened?"

She avoided his gaze. "Long, boring story. Not worth mentioning."

"Dropped it in the toilet bowl, then had second thoughts?"

"If I had, trust me when I say I wouldn't have bothered to replace it," she said tartly.

He grinned. Every now and then he caught a glimpse of her simmering temper, which meant she was probably keeping her full fury in check because of the bump she'd given him. There weren't any thrills in kicking a man when he was already down, so he was more than content to play the injured soul until she'd vented a portion of her pent-up anger.

"So what happened?"

"What's with the third degree?" she asked,

clearly exasperated. "It wasn't a priceless Ming vase, Adrian. It was a cheap toothbrush that you would have replaced in a few months anyway. You should be grateful I went out of my way to buy you a new one. I didn't have to, you know."

"I'm grateful. Really. It's just that I never knew you to be accident-prone."

Her face colored. "Yeah, well, life happens. Today just hasn't been my day. In more ways than one," she finished darkly.

He glanced around. "So where's my food?"

"I didn't order it in time to pick up before I came. They should deliver it before long."

"Good. I'm starved."

A baby giggled in the background, sounding as if it was right outside his room. "I didn't realize you admitted babies to this wing," he mentioned.

"Oh, we don't," she said lightly. "Peds is to the left of the elevators. You know how sound carries."

The baby cackled again. "This place has terrible acoustics if people can hear the kids throughout the entire floor," he said.

"He did seem close by," she admitted. "One of the nurses is probably walking around, trying to entertain a fussy one."

Her story didn't quite ring true. A nurse might

be strolling a colicky baby around the hallways, but she wouldn't expose an already sick infant to the germs on an adult ward. She would have remained on the pediatrics wing. Neither did it explain Sabrina's hurried glances toward the doorway, but at this moment, he had more important issues to tackle.

The infant's laugh suddenly became more of a shrill, happy scream. Adrian winced as the pitch caused his head to throb. "If that child is fussy, I'd hate to hear him when he's happy. In fact, he doesn't sound like a sick kid at all. Do they allow visitors to bring babies on to the floor?"

"Sometimes. Under extenuating circumstances." She rushed to close the door. "There. The noise shouldn't bother you now."

"I didn't say it bothered me," he protested.

"Whether it does or not, you need peace and quiet," she insisted. "And you really need to reconsider your decision to work tomorrow."

"I won't."

She muttered something about mule-headed doctors, then sighed. "I didn't think you would, even though we both know it's for your own good."

"I'm fine now and I'll be even better in the morning." He changed the subject, tired of having his health the sole topic of conversation. "I hear you're scheduled to work Emergency for the next month."

"Unfortunately, I am." She sounded resigned.

"Unfortunately?" He studied her closely. "Don't you like covering that department or are you afraid to work with me?"

"Afraid?" She sputtered, and bristled like a porcupine, which suggested he'd nailed the reason for her concern accurately. "I may not *want* to work with you, but I'm not afraid to. I'm a good nurse. A *careful*, meticulous, nurse. Just ask anyone. If you're not convinced, feel free to ask the director of nursing to reassign me while you're here," she finished caustically. "It wouldn't be the first time you pushed me out of your life."

He started to shake his head, then stopped as his skull protested. "Ask to reassign you? Not a chance."

"Oh, I get it. You're just planning to question my nursing skills and nitpick everything I do to death so that *I'll* ask for a transfer."

"I won't."

She eyed him dubiously and he continued, "Working together will be good for us."

Her jaw dropped. "You clearly need another CT scan. Your brain is obviously bruised."

Adrian laughed at her response. "I'm serious."

"So am I."

The apparently happy baby now yelled its rage so loudly Adrian heard him through the closed door.

"I have to go," she said instantly.

She couldn't leave yet! He hated the idea of spending the rest of the evening with only the television, his thoughts, and the eager-beaver nurses for company. More importantly, they hadn't had time to talk about his idea of starting over with a clean slate.

"What's the rush?" he asked. "It's still early. You can share my pizza."

"It's later than you think," she mumbled before she lifted her chin in defiance, "and I'm not hungry. Besides, I have things to do and…and someone's waiting for me."

The news caught him by surprise, although it shouldn't have. Bree, as he'd called her, always had a lot of girlfriends coming and going and he said so.

She bit her lip. "It's not a friend. He's my…guy."

He'd been celibate since their break-up and the idea of Sabrina having a relationship burned like a hot poker in his gut. After giving her the freedom to date someone else, his response was completely illogical. "Someone special?"

"Someone I love very much."

His spirits deflated like a punctured inner tube. It was depressing to think she'd moved on with her life so easily when he'd struggled. For now, he simply summoned a smile to hide his resentment and disappointment. "Be sure to introduce us."

"Yeah. Probably. Some day. I have to go."

"See you tomorrow."

"Right. Tomorrow."

Adrian watched her scurry from the room like a mouse escaping a cat before it could pounce. Sabrina had never been secretive before and if she'd been a typical woman scorned, she would have rubbed his face in the fact that she had a new man in her life. Yet she hadn't. She hadn't bragged or said anything about him—hadn't even mentioned his name—which seemed odd. In his experience, the women he knew never stopped talking about their latest love interest, whereas Sabrina had practically run away before she could.

Now that he thought about it, shouldn't she also have acted *grateful* toward him? After all, if they'd stayed together, she wouldn't have had the opportunity to meet this new man of her dreams.

Curiouser and curiouser.

Whether she had a boyfriend or not, he'd come to Pinehaven to do his job and salvage his career.

For the sake of everything he held dear—his profession and his family—he had to make his peace with Sabrina, then leave the past where it belonged.

You should have told him about Jeremy, Sabrina's alter ego scolded in the dark of the night, long after she'd finally tucked her son into bed. *You had the perfect opportunity.*

No, I didn't, she argued back. The perfect opportunity had been when she'd first learned she was pregnant, but at the time he'd still refused to talk to her.

In the days immediately after Clay's accident, she'd done everything she could to help Adrian and his family during their crisis. She'd sat by Clay's bedside so he wouldn't be alone, even though he'd been too groggy from pain meds to know she was there. She'd fixed meals for Adrian because he'd focused completely upon Clay to the exclusion of everything else. She'd run errands and washed a few loads of Adrian's laundry so he could spend more time with Clay. She'd understood his need as Clay's elder brother and head of the McReynolds family to be at the hospital every chance he could.

She'd also tried to be the emotional rock they'd

needed, encouraging them to think positive and not give up hope when the experts had admitted there was a chance that Clay might be a paraplegic.

Little did she know that this news became a turning point for her. Two days later, Adrian told her to stay away; he was ending their relationship because Clay required all his attention and energy. He didn't have room in his life for her, he claimed.

She argued her case that she could help, that she knew and understood how Clay was his priority, but he remained adamant. She begged and pleaded and told him how much he meant to her, but none of her entreaties made an impression.

He refused to reconsider. It was for the best, he told her.

From then on he didn't answer her phone calls, return her messages or speak to her in the hall. It was as if she had become a complete stranger.

Deciding she was only setting herself up for more pain, she changed her schedule so their paths couldn't accidentally cross, only visited Clay on a rare occasion when she knew Adrian wouldn't be there, and erased Adrian's number from her cellphone directory. Meanwhile, she prayed he'd come to his senses and kept her distance in every way possible.

Until the little test strip turned blue.

She waited outside the hospital after his shift had ended, hoping to catch him on his way to his car, but before she could rise off the park bench, a tall, beautiful redhead burst through the ER entrance doors and rushed after him. He turned, they talked, then he grabbed her close, swung her around with such exuberance that Sabrina could hear their laughter across the lawn.

His apparent no-time-for-romance philosophy only seemed to apply to her. Her spirits crushed, she slipped away before he could see her.

Pride stopped her from trying to contact him again. If he didn't have time for her, he certainly wouldn't have time for a baby. During her weak moments she debated about sending him a letter, but she was afraid his over-developed sense of family would force him to propose out of a mis-guided sense of obligation. She wasn't about to marry a man under those circumstances. After her mother had died, her uncle and his wife had taken her in because they'd felt they had to, and she'd been reminded of their sacrifice too often. Asking her child to suffer through the same was out of the question.

Another possibility was that he'd offer financial support, but strings always came with money.

She'd have to share her baby with him and she wasn't inclined to do that either.

He'd wanted to go separate ways, so she'd honor his wish. Having made her decision, she planned her future to become a single mom.

She arranged for a transfer to another hospital in the same consortium in order to maintain as many employee benefits as possible, announced her departure, hid her condition, which wasn't easy because she'd been so ill, then moved to Pinehaven to start over.

Now Adrian had arrived and no doubt would muck up her new life.

As she stared at the dark ceiling above her bed, she wished he'd never left Denver. The reasons for his arrival didn't matter, but what concerned her now was how he'd respond when he learned about his son.

Although Sabrina didn't expect Adrian to stay home the next day and give himself another twenty-four hours to recover, she hoped that good sense—or John Mosby—would rule the day. Unfortunately, Adrian reported for his shift bright and early at six a.m., looking quite strong for a man who'd spent the night in the hospital under observation.

"What are you doing here?" she asked as he

caught her reviewing the contents and arrangement of the trauma-room cupboards.

"My shift starts at six, remember?"

"I know that," she said stiffly, "but Dr Mosby couldn't have discharged you already. He doesn't make rounds this early."

"John called after you left last night. He said, and I quote, 'If you don't have any problems, you can leave first thing in the morning'. So I did."

"I doubt if he meant for you to check out before dawn."

"As far as I'm concerned, five-thirty can be considered 'first thing'. Just so you know, my vital signs passed muster all night, so after finding my way around the doctors' lounge to shower and change clothes, here I am."

And, indeed, here he was, wearing a long white lab coat over the pair of tan trousers and pale green dress shirt she'd delivered to him last evening. Surprisingly enough, he appeared well rested, which was hardly fair when *he* should have been the one to suffer a sleepless night instead of her.

He frowned as he studied her with similar intensity. "No offense, but you look more frayed around the edges than I do. A stiff wind would blow you away."

To think she'd spent extra time this morning with

her make-up to hide those dark circles under her eyes! She'd obviously wasted those minutes, along with her beauty products. As for the stiff wind, she'd lost all of her pregnancy weight and then some, because, for her, coping with a job and a newborn all by herself had been a terrific diet plan. Hating that he'd noticed, she changed the subject.

"I thought you're supposed to attend orientation this morning," Sabrina said, irritated because she had to share her first morning in the ED with him. As a floating nurse, it usually took her a day or two to fall back into the rhythm of her new assignment and she didn't want Adrian finding fault before she'd re-established an efficient routine.

"I am, but the session doesn't start until eight. I thought I'd orient to my own department before I learned about the rest of the hospital. So what's up?" He glanced at the board where all the current patients were listed, along with their preliminary diagnoses.

"As you can see, we're empty at the moment. This might be a good time for Hilary, our nursing supervisor, to give you the grand tour."

He grinned. "I already asked. She sent me to you."

"Oh, really?" Sabrina wasn't convinced.

"Yes, really. If you like, you can confirm it with her. She's in her office, mumbling about the schedule and sounding quite ferocious about staff hours and budget cuts."

"What about Dr Beth?"

"She's breakfasting in the cafeteria, or so I've been told."

In the time it took Sabrina to talk her way out of this little task or find someone else for the dubious honor, she could be finished, so she gritted her teeth and vowed to give him the fastest orientation in the ED's history.

"As you can see, this is the trauma room, complete with everything you could possibly need." Her gaze landed on the crash cart within easy reach.

"Our second trauma room is next door." She led him into the corridor. "And it can accommodate three patients, too. We also have six cubicles for walk-in patients and two that are set up for pediatrics.

"We have electronic record keeping, so all your reports can be found by accessing the hospital information system. I'm sure someone from IT will assign your password and explain how to navigate the software."

By the time she'd answered his questions, referred those she couldn't to Hilary and showed him around the entire department, it was time for his orientation session.

As soon as the double doors closed behind him, Sabrina sank bonelessly into a chair behind the nurses' station and rubbed the tense muscles in her neck. She'd known that working with Adrian underfoot would be tough, but these past two hours had been more difficult than she'd imagined. Not because he'd been rude or sullen or looked through her as if she didn't exist, but because he'd done the complete opposite! She didn't want him to be congenial, polite, or study her thoughtfully from under his incredibly long eyelashes.

She grabbed the receiver out of its cradle and prepared to dial her director of nursing when she suddenly hesitated. Asking for a transfer was like admitting to fear, and she wasn't afraid. She was anxious, wary, and cautious, perhaps, but she had faith in her abilities even though she had to work with a man who upset her composure just by standing in the same room. She would simply grit her teeth and suffer his presence for the next 3 weeks. After all, it wasn't for ever.

"You chose a good day to start in the ED," Hilary remarked as Sabrina joined her at the nurses' station.

Sabrina glanced at her supervisor, grateful that the woman was a congenial sort whose interest in her patients and staff was sincere. "How so?"

"It's a slow morning, our new defibrillator is on its way down from our bio-med department, and we have a new, handsome doctor in our midst."

"Oh, yeah. Right." Immediately, Sabrina felt Hilary's gaze rest upon her.

"You don't think the new guy is handsome?"

"Beauty, or handsomeness, is only skin deep," Sabrina returned.

Hilary chuckled. "You're too young to be so cynical, girl."

Sabrina grinned. "I am, aren't I?" Then, because she didn't want to discuss Adrian McReynolds, she asked, "Is there anything new I should know about?"

"Nothing I can think of at the moment, but feel free to read through our department manual."

"I will," Sabrina told her. She would do whatever was in her power so Adrian wouldn't find fault with her performance.

As it usually happened, their slow morning turned into a busy day and Sabrina could only spare those manuals a longing glance. A patient with a kidney stone was followed by a man who needed stitches after trying to sharpen his lawnmower blade by himself. After that came a chest-pain case, a teenager with strep throat, and an elderly man who'd fallen out of his bed at the nursing home and broken his hip.

Just as Sabrina was about to slip into the lounge and eat her late lunch, or early dinner, depending on how one described a mid-afternoon meal, a well-dressed woman in her sixties rushed through the emergency room doors, dragging two young children with her.

"Please, you have to help us," the woman begged as soon as she saw Sabrina.

Sabrina pushed aside her plans to put up her feet and enjoy her carton of yogurt. "What's wrong?"

"These two grandsons of mine…" the woman shook the arms of the two boys who stared at their surroundings with wide eyes "…got into my purse and ate my digoxin pills."

Sabrina immediately ushered them toward the pediatric trauma room, then flagged down the passing ward clerk. "Send Dr Beth, stat," she murmured before following them into the room where she hoisted each of the boys, approximately three and four years old, onto a bed. "How many did they swallow?"

"I just came from the pharmacy to refill my monthly prescription. There are only five left. Between the two of them, twenty-five are missing."

"And you're certain the boys ate them."

The woman nodded, her eyes frantic with worry.

"They were playing doctor. I don't know what possessed them to take the bottle from my purse. What's so awful is that I've always asked the pharmacy to use snap-on lips instead of the child-proof caps for my pills. You see, I live alone and my arthritis makes those lids difficult to open." She sniffled. "This is all my fault. I should have moved my purse or put my pills in the cupboard where they couldn't reach."

"Kids can get into trouble in the blink of an eye," Sabrina said.

The woman nodded, then squared her shoulders as if drawing on her emotional reserves. "As soon as I saw how many they'd eaten, I brought them straight here. If anything happens to Corey and Casey, I'll never forgive myself." Her voice cracked and her lips trembled. "I'm Edith Gilroy, by the way, and I'm watching my grandsons because my son and daughter-in-law are attending a funeral in Oklahoma City."

"We'll do everything we can," Sabrina told the trio as she began taking vital signs, noting the absence of any abnormalities.

"They look so healthy. Maybe those pills won't hurt them?" Edith asked hopefully.

"They will, I'm afraid. An overdose of digoxin

will produce cardiac toxicity which manifests itself in a number of ways, depending on the amount ingested. If we can get those pills out of their system before the drug is absorbed, they'll be fine."

Sabrina watched the two closely for the less serious symptoms of nausea, vomiting and a headache, hoping they could prevent the more severe ventricular tachycardia or fibrillation. So far, these two looked more scared than ill, although the time for symptoms to develop could be anywhere from thirty minutes to hours. Regardless, those pills had to be removed. By the time these two went home, they would never play doctor with their grandmother's medicine again.

"Should I have just gone to the drug store and given them syrup of ipecac?" Edith asked.

"No," Sabrina told her. "Vomiting can make any abnormal heart rhythms worse, which is why in cases of digoxin poisonings we often do a proce-dure called a lavage where we rinse out their stomach contents with fluids. Then we give acti-vated charcoal to adsorb any of the drug that may have gotten into the bowel."

"Oh."

When Adrian walked in as she finished her treat-ment overview, her surprised heart skipped a beat.

"What do we have?" he asked in the calm, quiet voice she remembered so well and had tried so hard to forget.

Wondering if he'd skipped out on his orientation class, she shoved her question aside to answer his. "Corey and Casey ingested a number of their grandmother's digoxin pills about thirty minutes ago." She glanced at Edith for confirmation and received it. "So far, they aren't showing any cardiac symptoms."

"And you're sure they swallowed them."

"I only have five left in my bottle," Edith interjected.

He turned to the two youngsters. "What were you boys doing?" he asked, while Sabrina worked in the background to retrieve the necessary supplies from the cupboards and shamelessly eavesdropped on his conversation with his little patients.

"Playin' doctor," the eldest said, his gaze intent on the stethoscope hanging from Adrian's pocket. "Are you a real one?"

Adrian smiled. "I am. And what did you do when you were playing doctor?"

"Corey here…" he glanced at his brother "…was pretendin' to have his arm broke and his throat hurt. I was goin' to give him a shot." He pulled a toy syringe from his pocket. "But he started to cry.

So I told him I'd give him pills like Mommy sometimes takes." Casey's lower lip turned into a pout. "I wanted to give him liquid in the alligator spoon like Mama uses, but Grandma doesn't have a spoon like that and her juice was all gone."

Edith gasped in the corner and Sabrina saw Adrian fight a smile at the boy's petulant tone.

"I'll bet the pills you found tasted nasty," he commiserated.

Corey shook his head. "Nope."

Sabrina exchanged a glance with Adrian. Digoxin tablets were tiny but, if chewed, were bitter. She couldn't imagine the boys gobbling them up and from the expression on Adrian's face he couldn't either.

"Then how did they taste?" he coaxed.

"Like apple sauce," Corey answered.

Once again, Edith moaned in the background, shook her head and covered her eyes.

"Apple sauce?" Adrian asked, clearly surprised.

Casey stared at him as if the man who towered over them should know that. "Mama puts pills in apple sauce, so that's what I did with the cups Grandma gave us for our snack."

"How many did you put in the cups?" Adrian pressed.

Corey held up two fingers. "Eleventeen."

The twinkle in Adrian's eye belied his serious expression. "That many," he said.

"I would have put more in, but Corey dropped the bottle and the pills rolled out. We tried to pick them up, but they were so tiny we just pushed them down the hole in the floor where the air comes out."

"The floor vent?"

"Yeah." Casey studied his shoe. "We didn't want Grandma to know we lost her pills 'cos she'd get mad at us."

"I see. How many went down the floor vent?" he asked. "A few or a lot?"

"Only a few."

"Did you eat any of the apple sauce, Casey?" Adrian asked.

"Not when I was the doctor. Doctors only give out medicine." He stared at Adrian as if he should know that.

"Did Corey pretend to be the doctor, too?" he asked.

Casey nodded. "My pills tasted like apple sauce, too."

Adrian turned to Sabrina. "It's hard to guess how many they ate and how many disappeared into the ductwork," he said wryly, "but we can't assume anything. Call in reinforcements so we can get started. I also want a baseline basic chemistry panel and digoxin levels on both boys."

A gastric lavage was the next step and with two patients they needed twice the number of hands. While Adrian explained the procedure of inserting a gastric tube into each boy's stomach in order to rinse out the contents, Sabrina recruited Dr Beth and Hilary to help.

Corey and Casey's blood samples were drawn and stomach contents flushed out until four of the missing twenty-five pills were accounted for—three from Corey and one from Casey—and the returned fluid ran clear.

Without a way to prove they'd removed all the medication, Sabrina administered activated charcoal, which the boys deemed "nasty" and refused to drink until Adrian warned them he'd insert the tubes again. Amid much gagging and misery, they complied. A laxative came next, which they downed most unhappily. While the two looked quite pathetic in their miniature hospital gowns as they waited dejectedly for the medication to send them to the toilet, Adrian called for the lab results and watched their heart monitors closely.

She'd expected him to pop in and out of the room, but he never left. He talked with the boys about television shows and the books their parents read. She was surprised to hear him recount the adventures of *The Berenstein Bears* and *Clifford, the Big Red Dog* as easily as he discussed cardiac arrhythmias. And when Casey began to retch, Adrian was there with a basin.

"Hey, now, buddy," he said as he patted the boy's shoulder. "I know this isn't fun, but it will be OK. I promise."

From Sabrina's position, she saw Casey's gaze meet Adrian's and an encouraging smile settled the deal. The youngster relaxed and all was well. From then on, whenever the children started to panic, he held hands, patted heads and shoulders, rubbed backs and told the occasional knock-knock joke to coax a smile.

The children kept him in their sights, as if he were their savior.

For a moment she pictured Adrian bouncing Jeremy on his knee, tickling his toes, and cradling him in his strong, capable arms. Until now, she'd justified her decision to keep her son's presence a secret, but years from now, when Jeremy asked about his father, would time prove her reasons to have been selfish? She'd ponder that question when she had a private moment.

Finally, she administered the digitalis-specific antidote. "Do you want to send them upstairs to Peds so they can monitor their drug and potassium levels?"

"I really think we flushed out their systems enough to avoid any problems, so if we have the bed space, let's keep them here for the next few hours," he said. And they did.

It didn't take long for the boys to get bored with only their grandma for company. When the latest lab results yielded numbers in the normal range, Adrian agreed to send them home.

"No more pills when you play doctor, OK?" he told the two sternly.

Both bobbed their heads.

"We don't want those tubes down our throats again," Casey assured him.

"Good decision. It wasn't fun, was it?"

"No. When I'm a real doctor, I can give pills, though, can't I?"

Adrian ruffled his hair. "You bet, but not until then."

Edith clasped his hand. "Oh, thank you for everything."

He smiled. "Just doing my job, but after meeting those two, I think yours is harder than mine."

She laughed. "Casey's definitely too smart for his own good, but trust me. I'll keep them on a short leash now."

After restoring the treatment room to rights, Sabrina's shift ended. As she headed for the exit, Adrian fell into step beside her. "Going home?"

"Yes," she said, feeling a little guilty for not admitting she was stopping by the hospital day care first.

"Do you have plans for dinner?"

She almost chuckled. Leftover tuna casserole and heating Jeremy's baby food didn't come close to the concept of "plans". Yet she knew where his question was leading. "I'm not interested in going out or having company."

"What about tomorrow night? I'll take you to dinner."

She shook her head. "Sorry."

"Thursday."

"I don't think so."

He frowned, clearly frustrated by her lack of cooperation. "You can't ignore me for ever, Bree."

"Oh, yes, I can," she retorted, meeting his gaze with a steely-eyed one of her own. "I learned how from a master. Goodnight, Adrian."

Unfortunately, as she reflected on the successes of the day, his kindness and concern for the two inquisitive and rambunctious boys gave her second thoughts about Adrian's request. No matter how hard she tried, she couldn't shake the picture of Adrian stroking Corey's hair or wiping the tears on Casey's face out of her mind. Was she doing the right thing by not telling him about Jeremy? Could she live with her decision?

On the other hand, and perhaps more importantly, could she share her son with a man she didn't trust? Considering how important family was to him, would he fight for custody, or would he decide he didn't have time for a son and leave the two of them alone?

She hoped for the latter because the possibility of losing her little boy was too frightening, too untenable to imagine, which was why she'd hadn't planned to inform him about Jeremy until he was at least eighteen. Unfortunately, with Adrian underfoot, she couldn't hide Jeremy's existence for more than a day or two. A conspiracy of silence involving all the hospital staff would never last for Adrian's tenure. Her only option was to break the news under her own terms.

As she reached the automatic doors, she realized that spewing caustic and bitter remarks just might make him defensive enough to fight her for custody on principle alone. Being congenial might go a long way to convince him to cooperate with her. She simply couldn't afford to antagonize him.

Resigned to being more amicable, she pivoted in his direction and tried to talk herself out of her impulsive decision.

He hadn't moved from the spot. She still could have stopped herself, but the bleak expression in his eyes melted the final strands of her resistance. She only hoped she could live with the consequences of what she was about to do.

"Friday," she said, aware that after he visited her house her life would change again. "You can come over on Friday."

His smile slowly grew wide, then he nodded. "Friday it is."

CHAPTER THREE

ADRIAN returned to the nurses' station with a definite spring in his step and a jaunty whistle on his lips. He'd survived his first day on the job with Sabrina and the day had gone far better than he'd hoped for or expected. Other than her obvious disdain when they'd been alone, they'd functioned as a cohesive medical team. Sheepishly, he admitted that he should have known she was a professional through and through, that she wouldn't be so petty as to allow their personal conflicts to interfere with the job.

In any case, come Friday evening, he'd find out if she was happy and had adjusted to her life. As much as he'd hated to let her go, knowing that his sacrifice hadn't been in vain would go a long way toward helping him find closure.

Hilary glanced up from her computer monitor. "You're in an especially jovial mood all of a sudden."

He smiled broadly. If the staff at Mercy Memorial had seen him, they would have wondered if he'd finally snapped. He hadn't earned the moniker of The Doctor To Avoid At All Costs by being a friendly sort over the past year. Now, being one step closer to mending his fences made him feel like the old Adrian McReynolds when everything in his life had been running as smoothly as well-maintained diagnostic equipment.

"I am," he admitted before he lowered his voice to a for-her-ears-only volume. "I have a date. With Sabrina."

Hilary stared at him as if he'd just sprouted an extra eye in the middle of his forehead. "You don't say."

"Yeah. Friday night."

"Wow. I'm impressed."

He was puzzled. "Why?"

"Because she doesn't date."

"She doesn't?" he said, wondering how the guy Sabrina had met last night after leaving him in his lonely hospital bed had fallen beneath her colleagues' radar.

Hilary shook her head. "Not that I've ever heard and, believe me, if she did, the news would travel faster than instant messaging."

"Are you sure?"

"Absolutely." She studied him closely. "You must have done something right if she accepted your invitation."

Actually, he'd done everything wrong, but the details weren't for Hilary's ears.

"I, for one, am glad she's finally willing to do something just for herself," Hilary continued. "She's a sweet girl and considering everything she's been through, there isn't a person in this hospital who doesn't want to see her happy."

Everything she's been through? What was Hilary talking about? Had she been ill? Could that explain her frail appearance, the tired circles under her eyes? It had been easier to think she'd simply moved away without incident. To hear otherwise would only drive a few more nails into his guilty conscience, but curiosity drove him to ask and caution warned him to brace himself for bad news.

"What has she gone through?"

"She's had a tough time since she got here, so if you cause her grief, you'll have a lot of folks who won't take kindly to you," Hilary continued, apparently choosing not to share specifics, which frustrated him to no end.

"I don't intend to cause problems."

"Good, because she doesn't need any right now."

Somehow, he felt as if he was missing an important piece of the puzzle, but he let that topic slide. "Are you certain she isn't seeing anyone? I could have sworn she'd mentioned something last night about meeting a guy." Someone she loved dearly, he recalled rather morosely, although he didn't know why the idea pained him when he'd wanted her to find a deserving fellow.

Hilary laughed. "She says that a lot to keep men away."

Hope sprang in his chest. "So there isn't a fellow in her life?"

She eyed him carefully. "By 'fellow', I assume you mean 'romantic interest'. If she did, she wouldn't have agreed to go out with you."

He grinned sheepishly. "I guess not." As it wouldn't hurt to ensure she didn't change her mind before their date on Friday, sending flowers might be a point in his favor. "By the way, she forgot to mention her address. Do you know where she lives?"

Apparently Hilary thought he was trustworthy, because she rattled off the location. "I can't remember the exact number, but she's in the housing development at the corner of Madison and Poplar. She has several potted plants on the front porch and a ladybug windsock hanging from the eaves. You can't miss it."

"Thanks."

Although he was eager to find a florist, duty tethered him to his post for another hour. Finally, after he'd completed his notes, he handed off the last patient—thirty-four-year-old Alan Cavendish who'd come in complaining of intense headaches, dizziness and nausea—to his evening shift replacement. Cavendish was already on his way to Radiology for an MRI and his blood tests were in progress. Dr Lehrer assured him he could handle the case from here, so Adrian gratefully left the hospital.

Driving down Central Avenue, he passed a grocery store sign that advertised a bakery, a hot food buffet, and a floral department. A quick decision sent him veering out of traffic into the parking lot. A few minutes later, he stood in front of the refrigerated case, studied the arrangements and debated between fresh flowers or potted daisies or carnations, a single bud or a bouquet. In the end, he asked the clerk for a dozen roses in assorted colors.

Impatient to see the look on Sabrina's face, he chose to deliver them now rather than wait until later in the evening. With luck, he might coax her into joining him for dinner tonight after all.

After punching the intersection Hilary had mentioned into his car's GPS system, he followed the directions. Five minutes later, the disembodied female voice announced he'd reached his destination.

However, as he gazed at the shabby duplex surrounded by several other equally shabby duplexes, he was certain he'd come to the wrong place. The peeling paint, sagging shutters, and yard that boasted more weeds and bare dirt than grass all testified that this was a low-income housing complex. He could only imagine what the inside looked like. Surely Sabrina hadn't moved *here*, had she? Nurses were paid well these days and he knew of her obsession with creating a nest egg for that proverbial rainy day.

If she lived here, her rainy day had clearly come and gone.

But rainy day or not, the ladybug wind sock that Hilary had described hung in full view above a potted plant. This was definitely Sabrina's place.

Determined not to judge by outward appearances, he strolled up the walk and knocked on the door. After a long minute without a response, he raised his hand to pound again when suddenly the door swung wide.

"Sorry to take so long," she said breathlessly, but her smile soon died as she remained framed in the entrance.

He'd expected to see her alone, not with a

gurgling baby on her hip. Immediately his dinner plans evaporated. "Hi," he said inanely.

"Adrian," she said, her eyes wide. "What are you doing here?"

He held out the roses. "After everything you did for me yesterday, I thought flowers were in order."

"Ah, thanks."

"Your hands are full," he said smoothly. "Why don't I bring them inside and help you put them in water?"

"Now isn't a good time," she began.

"Don't worry. I left my white gloves at home," he quipped, knowing how she hated visitors when her house wasn't spotless.

"Truly. I'm not prepared for visitors. Thanks for the flowers, though."

He should have left then and there, but he discovered that he couldn't. Seeing her in a pair of cutoffs and T-shirt with her hair loose and feet bare was a real reminder of the Sabrina he'd once known so well.

The baby on her hip began babbling, as if trying to talk, and Adrian stalled his exit for another minute. "Cute kid. From his blue romper, I assume he's a boy. What's his name?"

"Jeremy."

He tickled a spot under Jeremy's chin and elicited a hearty laugh. "So you're babysitting tonight."

She paused. "No. Jeremy is…"

Adrian glanced at her expectantly. "Jeremy is…what?"

"He's mine."

Words temporarily failed him as his head spun. "Yours? You have a baby?"

"Yes."

The news struck with the same impact as yesterday's golf ball and left him reeling. "How?"

She shrugged. "The usual way."

At first, he felt guilty because he'd obviously pushed her away and she'd found comfort in someone else's arms—someone who'd taken advantage of her, then left. But as he guessed Jeremy's age and mentally counted backwards, a sense of foreboding swept over him.

He stared at the child, this time seeing what he hadn't noticed before. Jeremy had the classic McReynolds chin, the same eyes and nose. In fact, he came close to looking very similar to himself in his own baby photos.

"How old is he?" he asked hoarsely.

"He's not quite seven months. He was born in January."

Still unwilling to believe his own suspicions, he met her gaze. "Is he mine?"

She squared her shoulders and lied. "No."

"Don't play games, Sabrina," he warned her. "He looks like the pictures of Clay and I when we were his age. I'm his father and don't deny it."

"Oh, all right. I'd like to say he isn't yours, but I can't," she snapped. "It's quite obvious just by looking at him that you were the sperm donor."

Hearing her confirm his status should have been a reassuring moment. Instead, Adrian's head felt as if he'd suffered another concussion.

He was a father. To a boy. A *son*. Another generation of McReynolds had arrived.

Immediately, he flashed back to the afternoon before his very first date with Marilyn Carstairs, a blonde who had been fifteen and built like she was twenty-five....

"I imagine you've learned all the physical mechanics of the birds and the bees by now," his father said.

"Yes, sir."

"There's a responsibility that comes with that sort of activity. Did your biology classes teach you that?"

Adrian met his father's sober gaze. "No, sir, but you have."

He nodded thoughtfully. "Keep in mind that ac-

cidents happen, no matter how careful a fellow tries to be. The best way to avoid it is to keep the horse in the barn, if you catch my meaning."

"I do."

"The consequences will last a lifetime," his father continued. "If there are any, a real man won't shirk his duty..."

He swallowed hard, shaken by his memory.

Sabrina peered at him, clearly concerned. "Are you OK?"

"I'm fine. Just surprised."

But other emotions soon followed. Anger that she hadn't told him she was pregnant. Guilt that she'd gone through her pregnancy alone. Fierce pride and joy that he had a son. Another bout of anger when he realized how easily he might never have known this earth-shattering piece of news. More anger as he reflected on how he'd heard his own child giggling and laughing last night and she'd refused to tell him. Refused to *introduce* them.

He purposely held onto his temper as he watched the baby that had instantly captured his heart with his chubby little face and drooling smile. Forcing his attention back to Sabrina, he saw her fearfully wide eyes. At the moment she had every right to be worried because this was a slight he couldn't forgive or ignore.

"Why didn't you tell me?" he demanded.

Ever since she'd collected Jeremy from the day care, Sabrina had agonized over her decision to tell Adrian about the baby they'd created. Her heart had told her it would be better if he heard the news from her because he'd find out anyway, but she hadn't forgotten those days when she'd had nothing but righteous anger to sustain her— when she'd been so ill with morning sickness and had worked her shift instead of curling into a fetal position and staying in bed; when she'd had to quit work a few months later and survive on her small nest egg and the generosity of others. Knowing Jeremy would be *hers* and hers alone until *she* said otherwise had given her a lifeline to hold onto when the world had seemed bleak and threatening.

Now her best-laid plans had vanished and she needed to devise a way to regain control of the situation.

"Why didn't you tell me?" he repeated.

"How? After our *enlightening* conversation, I rarely saw you and when I did, you weren't ever alone."

His jaw held a stubborn set. "You should have made the effort. Sent a letter. Done *something*."

"Done something?" she asked, incredulous. "You didn't answer my phone calls or respond to my emails. What would have been my clue that you would have welcomed a letter?"

He didn't answer, so she continued, clutching the flowers until she felt the thorns poke her palm through the protective plastic. "And why should I have bothered? You didn't have time for a relationship, you said, because you'd be too busy with Clay. Using your logic, if you didn't have time for me, then you certainly wouldn't have found time for a baby."

"A baby changes things," he insisted.

"Oh. So you're telling me now that after you'd decided you had too many demands on your time for me—an adult who helped you any way I could—you would suddenly have been able to share your free hours with a helpless baby?"

"You still…" He stopped in mid-sentence. "Can we take this inside or would you rather air our dirty laundry in public?"

As she sheepishly noted they hadn't moved off her front porch, she glanced toward the other half of her duplex and saw the curtains rustle. With a sinking heart Sabrina realized her neighbor was not only aware of their argument but had probably also heard the reasons for it. As a young mother who'd never had a single man darken her door since she'd moved in, the conversation that the elderly Mrs Owens overheard would end up as great gossip. Wordlessly, Sabrina stepped back and allowed him enough room to sidle inside her small home.

"Have a seat," she offered with chilly politeness as she motioned to the lumpy recliner that he probably remembered from their times together. It was one of the few pieces of furniture she still owned from her life BJ—Before Jeremy. She would have sold both it and the bed where she'd spent so many blissful hours with Adrian in her effort to wipe every trace of him out of her life, but she couldn't afford replacements.

Jeremy gurgled and blew bubbles, seemingly unaware of the undercurrents in the room, so she set him in his playpen with a few of his toys and hoped he'd continue to be more enthralled with his plastic rings than with the man who'd arrived.

She straightened to find Adrian slowly perusing her small living room, certain he noticed it only contained the recliner he was currently enjoying, a wooden rocker she'd bought at a garage sale, an umbrella stroller and a larger carriage, Jeremy's infant car seat, and a toy chest.

Even without her sofa, television, and other household effects, she'd taken pride in the cozy space she'd created, but Adrian's presence seemed to draw the walls closer and turn her haven into the size of a matchbox.

"Nice place," he commented.

"It suits us," she defended, well aware it didn't compare as favorably to her apartment in Denver, but this had been the only available apartment to fit her tight budget. "As you can see, I've decorated in Early Baby." Actually, she'd sold her own furniture to obtain the money to purchase the things Jeremy had needed, but Adrian didn't need to know that. She didn't want his pity.

"It's hard to believe one little person needs so much," he said simply.

"It is," she agreed, "but as one of my elderly patients once told me, 'Good or bad, this too shall pass.' I'm not as old as she was, but she made a believer out of me."

"For the record," he began, "when I broke off our relationship, I was trying to spare you."

"Spare me?" She stared at him, incredulous. "From what? From sharing my life with you when

I thought we'd enjoyed being together? From helping not just you but Clay, who was more than your brother to me? He was a *friend*."

He fell silent and when he spoke he'd softened his tone. "I saw everything you did for us and I appreciated it more than you know, but once I knew Clay would need extensive rehab, I had to give all of my time to him. You would have been tied to a man who simply couldn't be there for you."

"Did I complain?"

He fell silent.

"I understood what would be involved, Adrian. I didn't ask you to choose between romancing me and supporting Clay, did I?"

He hesitated. "No."

"You didn't have the right to make that decision on your own."

"It wasn't like we had made any promises to each other," he defended. "I was trying to do the honorable thing."

She raised her chin ever so slightly. "You failed. We may not have gotten to the point of being engaged, but if I hadn't lo—" She bit off the word *love* because she wasn't about to give him the satisfaction of knowing that she'd been head over heels for him. "If I hadn't felt something for you and thought what we had would continue to grow, I never would have slept with you in the first place. You, of all people, knew I didn't have indiscriminate or casual sex."

His skin turned ruddy, as if he'd conveniently forgotten that her first sexual encounter had been with him. A twenty-nine-year-old woman waiting that long for intimacy should have proved her character and established her principles.

"So, you see, Adrian, your brilliant idea to 'spare me' so I could create a wonderful life with a different guy who wasn't potentially saddled with a disabled relative was flawed from the beginning. If you ask me, you knew we had something good and suddenly got cold feet. Clay's accident just gave you the excuse you'd been looking for."

"No!" He shook his head. "No."

He sounded so horrified and so vehement that she might have been convinced had she not remembered the painful scene she'd witnessed. Unfortunately, nothing either of them said would be able to sway the other's opinion at this point. Replaying everything was only stirring up emotions that were better left at the bottom of the pot.

"Look," she said tiredly, "we can both rationalize and accuse and second-guess all we want, but it won't accomplish anything."

He frowned as he reached for the stroller parked beside him and rolled it back and forth. For a few seconds the only noises in the room consisted of Jeremy's gurgles and squeaky wheels. "I still wish I'd known you were pregnant," he said quietly.

His voice carried a wounded quality, as if he recognized exactly how much he'd lost by his magnanimous gesture and now regretted his choice.

"Just for the sake of argument, let's say you had known." She eyed him carefully for his response. "What would you have done, Adrian? Would you have had second thoughts or blamed me for getting pregnant? Or would you have felt guilty enough to marry me because it would have been the right thing to do? And if we had, would you have felt trapped?"

"No." He shook his head. "Never trapped."

His words were bitter-sweet, and suddenly she wanted to get everything out in the open, once and for all. "You say that now, Adrian, but I saw you with a redhead and she seemed quite important to you."

He appeared startled and a thought wrinkle marred his forehead. "A redhead? I don't know a redhead…"

"As a matter of fact, I *did* try to contact you. I waited outside the ER one night at the end of your shift. You had just come through the doors and were on your way to the parking lot when this woman ran after you. The two of you talked, then you hugged and kissed her before you swung her round and laughed as if you didn't have a care in the world."

To her surprise, mentioning what she'd seen was almost as painful as observing it for the first time. "You didn't have time for a romance with me," she continued, "but you obviously found the time to be with another woman."

He was clearly at a loss. "I didn't. There hasn't been anyone. You must have mistaken someone else for me."

She raised an eyebrow. "Then you have an identical twin who also owns the same green scrub suit with the bleached out spot on one pocket."

Still puzzled, he shook his head. "I don't remember…"

Somehow, his memory loss irritated more than it consoled or explained. "Did you go out with so many women that you've forgotten this particular lady?"

"No!"

He sounded so appalled she almost believed him, but the same pride that had stopped her from telling him about their baby rose again. "In any case, you'd obviously moved on with your life, so I made the choice to do the same."

"You didn't have to leave town."

"I wasn't a glutton for punishment, Adrian. I couldn't stay, but my transfer wasn't a secret." She met his gaze. "Considering how many months have passed, you can't claim you rushed to mend fences. Why did you come now?"

He leaned back. "My boss twisted my arm because I haven't been the easiest to work with. He thought I'd benefit from a change of scenery."

"Chewed out one too many nurses, did you?"

"Nurses, colleagues, it didn't matter. I was on the fast track to losing my position. As crazy as it sounds now, I was eaten up inside by not knowing how you were doing and I took out my frustration on my staff. I had to see you again, to reassure myself I'd done the right thing, but enough time had passed that I didn't know how to make the first move." He managed a smile. "As it happened, my boss took matters into his own hands.

"What's important now," he continued, "is that I *am* here, regardless of the how or the why."

She begged to differ. "If you say so."

"While I'll have to live the rest of my life with the reasons why you didn't tell me you were pregnant before you moved away from Denver, you could have told me about our son last night. The baby I'd heard outside my room *was* Jeremy, wasn't it?"

She heard the chiding note in his voice and it irritated her to think that he had the audacity to question her decisions when his own had been so faulty.

"Yes," she agreed defiantly, "but your head had just been sliced open by a golf ball, you had an entire drum corps pounding in your head and were under observation for a concussion. As I told you last night, you weren't in any condition to hold your end of a serious conversation and you certainly weren't able to handle additional shock and stress. In fact, I'm not sure you should be hearing this tonight, either."

"Believe me, *not* hearing this tonight would have been much worse." He paused. "Were you *ever* going to tell me about him?"

"I'd planned for the two of you to meet on Friday." At his dubious expression, she shrugged. "Believe me or not, I don't care. Introducing you to Jeremy was the only reason I agreed to see you. As for him being 'our' son, he isn't. He's *mine*."

"A judge might feel differently. Fathers have rights these days, too."

She squared her shoulders, raised her chin and bluffed. "Threaten all you want, Adrian, but intimidation won't work. I don't scare as easily as I did then."

This time, *he* bounded to his feet and rubbed his neck in obvious frustration. "Look, I don't want to fight about this. I'll admit I may have made a mistake—" At this she scoffed, but he continued, "But I don't want Jeremy to grow up with his parents at odds with each other."

Part of her wanted to rant over his naive belief that she could pick up where they'd left off on the strength of his I-may-have-made-a-mistake statement. The other part told her that carrying a grudge wasn't healthy for Jeremy, or for her. Frankly, she didn't have the energy required to fuel this level of animosity indefinitely.

"In my head, I know I should forgive you," she began tiredly, "and someday, Adrian, I probably will, but today my heart won't let me."

He accepted her reply with equanimity. "I'm asking for too much too soon, but I'll do whatever it takes to make it up to you."

She didn't think that would ever be likely, but his voice carried a note of promise, as if he was making a solemn vow to both of them. Before she could guess at or ask what he had planned, he spoke again.

"The big question at the moment is, what do we do next?"

His use of the plural pronoun irritated her. How like him to barge in and take over as if he were riding a white horse to the rescue!

"*We* don't do anything," she said firmly, determined to hold onto her position. "*I* will raise my son and you're welcome to visit him as long as you're in town. After you return to *your* family—" she couldn't resist throwing his long-ago reference back at him "—I'll drop you a postcard every now and then."

His eyes narrowed. "I want more than a postcard. Jeremy is part of my family, too. I'm as responsible for him as you are."

"No, you aren't," she argued. "You relinquished your claim a year ago."

"I. Did. Not!" he roared.

Jeremy immediately burst into a howl and Sabrina rushed to cuddle him against her chest. "Sorry, little man. He wasn't yelling at you, just at Mommy." She kissed the top of his head and wiped away the tears clinging to his eyelashes before she snarled at Adrian, "Would you please control yourself?"

To his credit, he appeared completely repentant. "Sorry. I didn't mean to shout."

Sabrina sat in the rocker, holding a wary Jeremy on her lap. "What if Clay suffers a relapse and he has to live with you so you can personally care for him again? I won't be put in the position of explaining to our son why his father doesn't want us except when it's convenient."

"It wouldn't be like that."

She turned a steely-eyed gaze on him. "Sorry, but I'm not convinced and I'm not willing to take the risk. For Jeremy's sake."

Jeremy began to fuss and the noise drew her attention as well as Adrian's as they watched the little boy, who'd suddenly become distracted by his bib and was currently stuffing the fabric into his mouth.

"Children need both their parents," he said simply. "I want Jeremy to know who I am."

"Certainly. Feel free to send a picture every now and again."

He shot her a look of disgust. "I'm supposed to be satisfied with Jeremy knowing me from a *photo*?"

"OK, fine. You can visit after you've gone back to Denver," she offered generously. "And I'd be happy to drop by whenever we head in that direction." Of course, she *never* drove near Adrian's house or Mercy Memorial and didn't intend to do so either. In fact, she hadn't traveled outside Pinehaven since she'd moved here.

"Not good enough, Bree," he said, unaware that his pet name for her irritated more than it soothed. "I can't be a face in a snapshot to him. I want to be his dad, in every sense of the word. Not just the sperm donor."

Obviously, her previous description had struck a sore spot in his ego. Studying him with suspicion, she said, "Your life isn't in Pinehaven, Adrian. How do you propose to be his dad when you're hours away?"

"I don't have specifics," he said, clearly exasperated. "If you recall, I haven't had a lot of time to digest the fact that I have a son. But I can tell you this. Being an absentee father isn't in my plans and I'll do whatever it takes so it doesn't happen," he said grimly, as if preparing himself for battle. "I'll drive back every weekend if necessary."

She shouldn't have been surprised by his offer. His strong sense of family had cemented her attraction to him long ago, but she'd hoped Adrian's animosity toward her would be enough to convince him to maintain his distance.

"You can't have one of us without the other," she

said firmly. "I'm not going to turn Jeremy over to you whenever you roll into town. Nor will I send him back and forth between our homes like a package, so don't waste your time suggesting it."

"You may not have a choice."

She met his gaze. "If you want to fight this, I will." She didn't know how or where she'd find the money if he pursued legal action, but she would.

To her surprise and relief, he backed down. "Let's not overreact. I've only known of Jeremy's existence for..." he glanced at his watch "...two hours. Logistics and legalities can come later."

Meaning that at some point in the relatively near future he wouldn't be satisfied with hovering on the fringes of Jeremy's life. As she wasn't willing to share, a no-win situation loomed.

"While I'm in town, though," he continued, oblivious to her thoughts, "I intend to catch up on everything I missed."

She could either cooperate or not, but his demand made it plain that one way or another he wouldn't be thwarted. Unfortunately, sharing her son with Adrian was easier said than done.

"Catching up on Jeremy's short life is impossible tonight," she said, flatly. "It's getting late, I haven't eaten all day, and it's time for Jeremy's bath."

He didn't move. "I know I'm wearing out my welcome, but I'd like to stay and help with his nighttime routine. I promise not to get in the way or disrupt your schedule."

"You already have."

"Probably," he agreed, "but…please?"

Months ago, she would have been happy to hear Adrian beg, but seeing him humble himself as he already had several times tonight only made her uncomfortable. She had enough faults without adding cruelty to the list. Besides, what would it hurt? If cooperating now meant he wouldn't fight for custody later, then she would.

"You'll get wet," she warned. "'Splash' is Jeremy's middle name." Adrian's subsequent grin reminded her of happier times when her future had seemed safe and secure in his hands. She pushed aside those bitter-sweet memories.

"I won't melt," he promised, rising to stand beside her.

As difficult as it was for her emotionally, she placed Jeremy in Adrian's arms, careful to avoid physical contact because she didn't want to remember how good it had felt when he touched her. Stepping back, she watched him hold their son like the priceless treasure he was.

The awe in Adrian's eyes and in his expression as he gazed at his bundle brought a lump to her throat. She saw his steady hand tremble as he caressed Jeremy's cheek and touched his tiny fingers. Jeremy stared at him in silent wonderment, as if he instinctively sensed the connection between them.

She held her composure until Adrian's eyes developed an unmistakable sheen.

"Bring him into the kitchen when you're ready," she said hoarsely before she fled. She was generously giving them a moment alone to meet each other, she told herself as she plucked Jeremy's bath towel and washcloth off the rod in her bathroom. It had nothing to do with the emotional moment of a father holding his son for the first time.

As she passed through the living room on her way to the kitchen, the sound of Adrian's baritone almost undid her as he sang a child's verse about the things Papa would buy him. What hurt worse was how Jeremy gazed at his father with undivided attention and a toothy smile, as if he loved hearing this new and more interesting voice than his mother's.

Sharing her flesh and blood with a man she couldn't trust had become even more difficult that it had a few minutes ago. She wanted to snatch Jeremy away because Adrian didn't deserve such instant and unconditional adoration, but she couldn't. She'd suffer through, for Jeremy's sake.

She should be thrilled Adrian would be a part of Jeremy's life because her son wouldn't grow up without knowing his father. She should be ecstatic at the prospect of sharing the responsibilities of raising a child. She should feel vindicated that Adrian wanted to make amends and had admitted his mistakes, but she didn't feel any of those things. She only felt empty inside.

He was beautiful, Adrian decided as he cradled Jeremy against him, handling his little body for the first time. He was disappointed for missing out on Jeremy's first months, but he couldn't blame anyone except himself. If he hadn't been so eager to put his life on hold to ease his guilt over Clay's accident, things would have turned out differently. He never should have loaned him the money to buy the motorcycle in the first place, but Clay had set his heart on one in spite of Adrian's warnings about the inherent dangers. So he'd given in and his worst fears had come to pass.

Determined to appease his conscience, he'd focused on Clay at Sabrina's expense. Now he had to save Sabrina from making his mistake. Contrary to what she might believe, pushing him away as he'd pushed her wasn't in anyone's best interests.

Part of him wanted to appeal to the court system and force her to give him a piece of Jeremy's life. Unfortunately, doing so would alienate her and place Jeremy in a position where he'd feel disloyal if he loved both his parents. His best option was to stay calm and cooperate with her so she didn't feel threatened. Once the pain of their past faded, they could readdress the visitation issue.

As Jeremy stopped chewing on his fist to gaze at him with complete trust, Adrian's chest swelled with love and commitment. "Your mom and I are going to work this out. One way or another. I promise."

Jeremy grunted and Adrian kissed his forehead, reveling in his baby scent. "Come on. Your mom's waiting."

He carried him into the kitchen and ten minutes later, as Sabrina had predicted, most of Adrian's clothes were soaked.

She smiled as she wrapped Jeremy in a bath towel. "I told you so."

"I'll wear swim trunks next time."

"That won't be necessary," she said quickly, as if she remembered what had happened the last time they'd both worn bathing suits. "Just wear old clothes."

He grinned inside, pleased she was giving him another opportunity to take part in Jeremy's evening routine.

"I'll slip on his pajamas if you'll warm his bottle." She pointed to the stove as she stood poised in the doorway. "It's in the refrigerator, ready to go."

He eyed the pot of water on a front burner. "Will do, but don't you think it's too hot for jammies?" The room's temperature was definitely warmer than what he considered comfortable, and he had the added bonus of having damp clothing to cool his overheated skin.

"He wears a diaper and a T-shirt," she called over her shoulder, "not footed flannel sleepers."

He opened the fridge and found the bottle, then paused as he noted the sparse contents. A few apples, a bag of carrots, a carton of eggs and a near-empty quart jug of milk didn't come close to filling the space. Just thinking of food made his stomach growl a reminder that he hadn't eaten, either.

Quickly, he closed the refrigerator to conserve its cold air, plunked the bottle inside the pan and set the water to boil, then called in a pizza delivery order courtesy of a number he found in the phone book. With their upcoming meal under control, curiosity drove him to check out her cupboards. Their sorry state matched the refrigerator's.

Before he could snoop around a bit more, the bottle was ready and Sabrina appeared in the doorway with Jeremy gnawing frantically on his hands and smacking his lips. "How are you coming?" she asked as she bounced him on her hip.

He shook a few drops of formula on his wrist. "I guess this is warm enough. Want to check for yourself?"

She did, then pronounced it acceptable. "Would you like to feed him?"

He heard a trace of reluctance in her voice, as if she hoped he'd refuse, but he couldn't. "I'd love to."

Once again, she handed Jeremy into the crook of his arm, but this time his fingers brushed against the soft swell of her breast and she gasped. Afraid to move for fear he'd drop the baby, he froze.

Immediately, blood rushed to his groin and his body responded as if they hadn't spent the last year apart. Saints in heaven, he'd missed the feel of her skin against his, the way her fingertips had glided across his abdomen, the sensation of taking her in his mouth and driving her wild.

She moved just enough to break contact. "Do you have him?"

The breathless quality in her voice suggested that the accidentally intimate touch had rekindled those memories for her, too.

"Yes," he said, hoping she wouldn't notice how his trousers had suddenly tented.

"Take the rocking chair. And be sure you burp him every few ounces because he feeds too fast. If you don't, we'll be giving him another bath," she advised wryly, "and you'll be wearing 'eau de formula'."

Adrian obeyed. Silently and under Sabrina's watchful eye, he fed and dutifully burped as instructed. Apparently satisfied by his efforts, she eventually disappeared into the kitchen. He was flattered that she trusted him, but the bleakness in her eyes suggested another reason. Perhaps she couldn't sit by and watch the man who'd rejected her so completely fall instantly and irrevocably in love with their son.

He may have wedged his size eleven foot in the proverbial door to get this far, but he had a lot of penance to complete before he could step inside.

Jeremy had emptied the bottle and was asleep by the time she returned.

"What now?" Adrian whispered.

"Lay him in his crib," she answered. "It's in my bedroom."

He followed, loath to let the little boy out of his arms, although he couldn't and shouldn't hold him all night.

Just as he was about to lower Jeremy onto the mattress under Sabrina's watchful eye, the doorbell awakened Jeremy. He wrinkled his face and screwed his mouth into a wail.

"Who's that, I wonder?" Sabrina spoke in a near whisper.

He kept his voice low, too. "Probably the pizza I ordered."

She stopped in her tracks. "You ordered pizza?"

Adrian heard the surprise and displeasure in her voice over Jeremy's unhappiness. He shrugged as he soothed the baby against his shoulder and tried to console him with a pacifier. "What can I say? I was hungry and I assumed you were, too."

She lowered her gaze to a point somewhere near his breastbone. "I…um, I can't pay him."

"I didn't expect you to feed me," he told her. "My billfold's in my hip pocket. Take what you need." He turned to give her easy access.

She gingerly removed the wallet, as if she was afraid to touch him, then disappeared. As he crooned softly to Jeremy and the youngster settled down once more, Adrian studied the room. Zoo animals dotted the bedding and a mobile featuring similar creatures hung from the headboard. The rest of the room was filled with more baby paraphernalia, a small dresser and her bed.

Jeremy seemed to own all the equipment necessary for a baby, but Sabrina definitely lived a spartan existence. Before he had a chance to work the inconsistency out in his mind, she reappeared.

Without his wallet, he noticed wryly. Clearly, she didn't want to return it to the place where she'd found it, although he'd rather hoped she would. He missed her touch, even as impersonal as it would have been.

"Is he asleep?" she asked.

"I can't tell for sure, but he hasn't moved, so I think he is."

Ever so gently, he placed Jeremy on his back and covered him with a light cotton sheet. For a long moment, he stared down at the miracle of his son.

Unable to stop himself, he snaked his arm around Sabrina's waist and pulled her close, allowing himself a few seconds to revel in the moment. "Thank you," he whispered.

"For what?"

"For having him," he said simply. "Under the circumstances, it would have been easier to choose another option. I'm so glad you didn't."

Her smile wobbled as she gazed at the tiny figure in the crib. "There wasn't another option," she said simply. "He was all I had."

CHAPTER FOUR

ADRIAN had always prided himself on achieving his goals, but his success at pushing Sabrina out of his life so she could have a clean start had been an expensive accomplishment. The experiences he'd lost as a result were priceless. All these months, he'd imagined her happy, prosperous, and relieved that she'd escaped a half-hearted relationship. Instead, he'd found her struggling on her own to maintain a home and a job as well as being a single mother to *his* son.

Oh, yes. His so-called victory was hollow indeed.

He tightened his grip on her waist to hug her. How could he ever undo the damage? It was obvious from their earlier conversation that he could talk until he'd used his last breath, but words wouldn't heal her mistrust. Action was the only thing he had left to prove he'd changed.

However, as he gazed down at her, his intention to devise a strategy faded. If the anguish on her familiar, pixie-like face had haunted him before, he'd never be able to sleep again after seeing her somber expression or her pain-filled eyes. Her mouth trembled, drawing his attention to those sweet, warm, moist lips that had always driven him wild.

He wanted to kiss her, to "make it better", as his mother had always done whenever he'd sported a new scrape or a painful bruise. Before he could debate the pros and cons of taking the liberty, he simply took it. He lowered his head and gently brushed his lips against hers.

Nothing happened. Just when he was ready to concede defeat, her lips parted. As he hauled her closer, he sensed her rising on tiptoe to meet him.

Aware of her response and gratified by it, he continued his light pressure, knowing she was near tears and hoping his non-verbal apology could stem the oncoming tide.

Slowly but surely, her response changed, as if she'd understood and accepted what he was trying to say without words. Her hands slowly came up to rest on his chest and she molded her mouth to his.

An instant later, she jerked herself free, horror written on her face. "We can't. No." She shook her head and took a step back. "This doesn't solve anything."

Not everything, he mentally agreed, but in his opinion they were certainly heading down the right path. "I know it doesn't," he admitted, "but—"

She rushed out and he followed her to the center of the living room where she stood with her arms folded around her as if she'd drawn inside herself.

"Why did you come?" she asked in a trembling voice. "Why couldn't you have stayed away?"

"Because—"

As if she'd gathered every bit of strength from within, she squared her shoulders and her eyes flashed fire. "You need to go. Out of my house. Out of my hospital. Out of our lives!"

"I know this is tough—"

"You have no idea," she said bitterly.

"But it isn't easy for me, either. I'd go if I could, but I can't, Sabrina," he said flatly. "Not after knowing we made a beautiful boy. Don't ask that of me because I can't give you what you want. I just can't."

I can't give you what you want.

Adrian's comment echoed through Sabrina's head as he waited for her reply. Given his sense of responsibility and his devotion to family, she truly hadn't expected him to walk away so easily. Neither would he be satisfied with her doling out Jeremy's time with an eyedropper. Unfortunately, although she'd suspected he'd respond exactly as he had, she'd *hoped* he'd do the opposite.

She chewed nervously on her lip, resigned to the prospect of his steady presence and taking an active role with their baby while he fulfilled his contract in Pinehaven. However, it was anyone's guess what he might do or want after he returned to his position in Denver. For a while he'd probably phone every evening or organize weekend excursions. He might even set up one of those webcams in order to see Jeremy in real time as he talked to him, but the novelty of being a long-distance parent would wear off as soon as he got tired of dealing with the logistical problems. Or so she hoped.

Until then, though, he'd be underfoot. What she truly hated about having him in her home on a regular, if not daily basis, was that she wasn't as immune to him as she'd believed. At the moment she didn't know if she was upset with him for kissing her or upset at herself for responding.

She tucked a loose strand of hair behind her ear with a shaky hand. "I had to ask."

He nodded, as if he understood how desperately she wanted her life back—the life she'd had before he'd rolled into town. "As long as you know I'm in this for the long haul, we're both on the same page."

"And how long will that be?" At his protest, she held up her hands. "It's a fair question. I thought we were in a relationship for the long haul, too, and we both know how quickly that changed."

"Nothing, short of my death, will keep me away."

It was a vow, she sensed, spoken firmly and with sincerity. One thing she knew about Adrian—when he committed to something, nothing would sway him from his decision. Whether that character trait was a positive one or was a flaw, his set jaw and determined demeanor telegraphed how completely immovable he was on this subject.

If she had to surrender this battle, she would surrender under her own terms.

"All right, but we need a few ground rules," she told him, noticing how the tension seemed to leave his shoulders and relief appear in his eyes, as if he'd expected more of a fight. "We've both seen or known families torn apart by strife and I don't want Jeremy to live in the same state of uncertainty when we're together."

"Neither do I."

"And no more of what just happened in my bedroom. We both reacted to the emotional moment. That's all it was," she insisted. "I'm not interested in picking up where we left off before Clay's accident. The relationship we once had is over."

He opened his mouth as if to protest, but she glared at him. "OK," he said. "We'll take that as it comes. Anything else?"

"No."

"Good. Then let's eat."

Eat? He wanted to *eat*? The knots in her stomach made it impossible to digest food. "I'm really not hungry—"

"I ordered your favorite. Pepperoni and mushroom."

He'd remembered her weakness. She might have been able to resist the temptation, but she hadn't indulged in the extravagance in a very long time because her budget didn't cover such luxuries, and the scent alone was causing her mouth to water.

"Come on," he coaxed. "We're starting over, remember? Most dates involve a meal where the two people can talk and get to know each other."

"We aren't dating."

"Whatever. Regardless, we're going to spend a

lot of time together unless you're willing to let me take Jeremy back to my place."

She snorted. "As if."

"I thought not, which means it will be very awkward if we only talk to Jeremy. Eventually, he'll wonder why his parents never say more than two words to each other."

Years would pass before their son would notice that sort of detail, but as someone had once said, "A journey begins with a single step." So she might as well begin hers now. For Jeremy's sake.

"OK, I'll share your pizza, but then we'll have to call it a night. My shift starts early in the morning."

"Fair enough."

They sat down at her kitchen table where she'd covered most of the scratches, knicks and gouges under the cheery yellow sunflower place mats she'd sewn, and he began firing questions with a boyish eagerness that brought a smile to her face.

"Tell me about your pregnancy. How was your labor and delivery? Has Jeremy changed a lot since he was born? Do you have photos?"

"We agreed to catch up tomorrow," she reminded him.

"I know, but I can't wait. Surely you can share a few things," he coaxed.

She hesitated. Waiting another day wouldn't change anything and Jeremy *was* her favorite topic of conversation, so she bowed to the inevitable. After all, cooperating with Adrian would only serve her best interests, she reminded herself for the umpteenth time.

Choosing to answer his last question first, she said, "Of course I have pictures. I have them in the other room." Carrying her pizza slice with her, she located an album on a shelf in the living room and carried it to the table. "Here. Take a look."

Immediately, he stopped eating to open the padded book. Reverently, he turned the pages, stopping at several to comment. Surprisingly enough, he paused at the images taken at her baby shower. "You didn't gain much weight," he remarked.

She hadn't. For starters, she'd been so ill up to her fifth month that her obstetrician had threatened to admit her to hospital. And after that she'd developed high blood pressure, which heralded pre-eclampsia. Although she'd cut back her hours to part-time work, eventually her condition had progressed to the point the doctor had prescribed bed rest. Fortunately, Jeremy had decided to arrive two weeks early, otherwise Dr VanderWaal would have performed a Cesarean section.

"I got fat and waddled like every other expectant mom," she said lightly, hoping he wouldn't notice she hadn't shone with the expected glow of impending motherhood. She'd been allowed out of bed for her two-hour party and then, like clockwork, Kate had driven her home. While she'd rested, her friends from the hospital had carried in all the presents and stowed everything away.

He frowned as he studied the snapshots. "You look pale. Were you anemic? Did your doctor prescribe vitamins? Better yet, did you take them?"

"You can't diagnose me from a photo taken in bad lighting," she protested, although she hadn't looked her best that day. "I did have a few problems, but they all worked out. As for labor, it went fairly quickly. One of the OB nurses, Kate— she golfed with me yesterday—acted as my coach.

"Anyway." Her voice softened as she reflected on those hours after his birth. "Jeremy was this tiny baby with a few strands of the darkest hair." She flipped another page and pointed. "See?"

Adrian groaned good-naturedly. "Someone curled it. Who would do such a traumatic thing to a boy?"

"Kate. She thought it made him look cute—more like a baby and less like a little old man. Everyone remarked on how he seemed to know what people said to him, probably because he always looked directly at the person talking."

"Intelligence shows." He grinned. "He gets that from his dad."

"He definitely inherited your disposition," she said wryly. "He's easygoing until he wants something, and then you'd better give it to him right away, or else. As small as he is, he doesn't mind throwing his weight around."

His skin turned ruddy. "We'll have to work on that together." His watch beeped the hour and he frowned as he checked the time. "I guess that's my cue to go," he said, clearly reluctant to cut short their evening.

"Take the album with you," she said magnanimously. "If you'd like copies of the photos, I saved them to a CD so you can make prints. I put the camera you gave me for my birthday that year to good use."

"I'm glad."

"Oh, and speaking of gifts…" She hurried into her bedroom, rummaged through her sock drawer, and returned with the tiny box containing an expensive diamond pendant in a double-heart design that he'd given her for Christmas. "I almost forgot. This is yours."

He stared at the jeweler's box as if it were a canister of anthrax, then met her gaze. "You should keep it."

"What for?"

He shrugged. "Save it for Jeremy."

"No, thanks." She reached out, grabbed his hand and placed the case in his palm. "Please take it. I have no use for a necklace like this. If I should ever meet anyone else, I'd feel too awkward to ever wear it."

"Keep it," he repeated.

She held up her hands and backed up a step, out of arm's reach. "I should have returned it before I left Denver, and I would have but… Anyway, just take it. Give it to your…to someone else who'll appreciate it."

In her dreams, she'd always imagined herself handing the gold pendant to him as carelessly as if it were a piece of costume jewelry. In real life, however, transferring ownership hadn't been as satisfying as she'd imagined. Perhaps she should keep it—for Jeremy—but the necklace was simply too painful a reminder to accidentally run across. The interlocking hearts had seemed so appropriate but apparently she'd read far more into the meaning behind the design than Adrian had. To her, the shape had been a sign of their feelings for each other, while to him it had meant nothing. Removing the pendant from her drawer only marked The Official End to a relationship that had precipitously ended a year ago.

Instead of feeling liberated and relieved, she felt…lost and depressed, which was ridiculous. Disposing of this gift was supposed to be part of the healing process. Wasn't it?

His fingers closed over the small square box and he slipped it into his pocket. "Do you need anything? Anything at all? Anything like…" He glanced around the room as if searching for ideas, "I don't know, formula or baby stuff, or even a sofa?"

"Jeremy and I are fine. We don't need a thing," she said firmly.

"I feel as if I owe you something."

How typical to think money would solve their problems when it would only ease his conscience. "You don't."

He looked thoughtful, but didn't argue. Thank goodness, because she wasn't ready for a full-scale argument. He only said, "If you don't mind, I'll check on Jeremy one more time and then I'll get out of your hair."

"OK."

He didn't stay long in Jeremy's room and left after delivering a curt "See you tomorrow". After she'd closed the door behind him, Sabrina tidied her tiny home and removed all traces of their impromptu dinner. However, as the pizza scent lingered in the air after she'd stuffed the box in the trash can outside, so did the memories of his strong, steady embrace and the kiss that had curled her toes and reawakened her hormones.

She couldn't forget the instant when he'd splayed his hand across her back to anchor her tightly against him or how her own body had betrayed her as she'd risen on tiptoe to meet him halfway. Luckily, her good sense had kicked in and stopped her from allowing the situation to escalate. They'd only been reacting to the emotional moment, she told herself for the tenth time. As sizzling as the kiss had been, it didn't mean anything.

How embarrassing to think that even with their history she still responded to his touch and his non-verbal signals so easily. How pathetic was that? Pathetic enough to wish for a carton of either fudge ripple or chocolate chunk ice cream to magically appear in her pitifully empty freezer.

Over the next couple of days, in spite of berating herself for being so weak, in spite of Adrian sub-sequently acting like the perfect gentleman, or perhaps *because* he acted like the perfect gentle-man, those living color memories resurfaced at the oddest times. Like now, when she should be con-centrating on Mrs Gardner in room four.

The woman had come in with sudden indigestion when she hadn't eaten for hours, a squeezing sensation in her chest that continued into her throat and both jaws. Although the symptoms weren't typical for a heart attack, Adrian seemed in favor of the diagnosis after reviewing her EKG. Now Sabrina was checking the computer for the lab's cardiac enzyme results and waiting for a cardiologist to arrive.

"Yo, there, Sabrina." Hilary bustled up to the other side of the counter. "If you're relatively caught up, I want you to handle the walk-in we're getting. A woman was found wandering the streets, confused and possibly assaulted. The cops are bringing her in."

"No ambulance?"

"The paramedics are tied up at a warehouse fire, so the police decided not to wait for them."

The automatic ambulance bay doors opened and two uniformed officers escorted a petite woman inside. "They're here," Hilary announced. "I'll find Dr McReynolds and send him in ASAP."

Sabrina strode toward the trio, noting the woman's bloodied face, torn clothing, and the way she clutched the blanket around her as if it were armor. "I'm Sabrina," she said gently as she touched the woman's shoulder to guide her into a nearby exam room. "I'm going to be taking care of you. Meanwhile, would you like me to call your family, or a friend?"

The woman simply stared at her with panic in her eyes. "I don't—I can't…"

"We don't know who she is," the middle-aged Officer Malone, according to his nametag, volunteered. "The victim says she can't remember her name. You don't by any chance recognize her, do you?"

Sabrina studied the thirty-ish brunette's battered features. When the swelling subsided and the bruises faded, she'd be quite attractive. "Sorry."

"We're hoping you folks find a distinguishing mark or two to help ID her if anyone files a missing persons report."

"I'll see what I can do." She closed the door behind them and coaxed her to release the blanket.

The woman's clothes, although torn and bloody, were of a much higher quality than most. Her neck sported a number of red marks, suggesting someone had ripped off her necklace. Her hands were devoid of all jewelry, although her left hand's ring finger showed a distinctive band of white.

Helping her into a hospital gown was like helping

a two-year-old. The woman had definitely been traumatized.

"Why can't I remember? I want to," the woman said on a near sob. "I remember being in a car and then walking, so I should be able to think of my own name, but when I try, my head hurts."

"You have a nasty bump," Sabrina told her kindly. "Sometimes those injuries can cause temporary amnesia."

"How long is 'temporary'?"

"It depends," Sabrina prevaricated. "A neurologist can give a better answer than I can. Meanwhile, you simply have to give yourself time to heal, both physically and emotionally. You never know when a conversation, a sound or a smell might trigger your memories."

"I suppose." She didn't sound convinced.

"First things first," Sabrina declared. "Have you eaten?"

The woman shrugged. "I don't know. I think so. Whether I did or not, I'm not hungry."

"A snack always helps," Sabrina told her. "After the doctor is finished, I'll scrounge something from the cafeteria. Maybe soup or a sandwich, along with tea or coffee. Or does a soda sound better?"

"Cherry cola would be nice. It's my favorite." Her face lit up as soon as she spoke, then her smile became a frown. "How can I remember what I like to drink when I can't remember who I am?"

"The mind does unusual things during times of intense stress," Sabrina said. "The good thing is that you *are* remembering little details. Chances are good the rest of your memory will return soon. As I said, the specialist will be able to answer all of your questions." She took her clothes and placed them in a proper bag to be used as legal evidence.

Adrian walked in at that moment, along with a striking blonde in her forties who wore a police badge. "I'm Dr McReynolds," he said in a low, soothing voice, "and this is Detective Harper. If you're ready, I'm going to examine you and then you can shower and change clothes. Sabrina will find something for you to wear."

He raised an eyebrow at Sabrina and she nodded. They stored a few scrub suits for occasions like this.

The brunette's mouth quivered. "Thank you."

He gently examined her as Sabrina stood by and noted her injuries. In addition to the obvious scrapes and contusions, she had distinct marks on her arms, indicating that at least one person had grabbed her. Two of her ribs were separated—fortunately, neither had punctured a lung—and an angry-looking cigarette burn marred her left thigh.

As Adrian performed a pelvic exam, his sober glance at Sabrina said it all. The woman had been sexually assaulted.

In his quiet baritone, he explained everything he was doing while Sabrina carefully labeled the samples he'd collected. Detective Harper's sharp-eyed gaze followed the proceedings as she murmured encouraging words to the victim.

In a remarkably short amount of time they'd finished treating her injuries, obtained blood and urine samples to check for medical conditions, and administered the appropriate prophylatics to guard against HIV and hepatitis. The only real surprise was that Jane Doe's pregnancy test result had come back positive.

"The real kicker is that she probably wouldn't have known even if she hadn't lost her memory," he remarked after they'd sent her to X-Ray for chest films. "Her beta-HCG level is very low, which suggests she's only days into her pregnancy."

"Will she miscarry?"

He shrugged. "We wait and see."

"What will happen in the meantime? We can't discharge her when she can't fend for herself."

"We won't," he promised. "I'll admit her for observation because a concussion could have caused her memory loss. With luck, the police will locate someone who knows her before being homeless becomes an issue."

"I saw the white line on her finger. Whoever hurt her probably stole her wedding ring."

"That's my theory, too. According to the police, she was wandering around in a residential area, probably trying to get home."

Sabrina nodded. "I should have asked Officer Malone what they'll do to find her family."

"If no one files a missing persons report, they'll look for abandoned cars."

"What if the bad guy stole that, too? Or if she walked?"

"Then they may issue a press release asking the public for information."

"And if no one comes forward and we can't find a reason to keep her?"

"I imagine she'll go to the local women's crisis shelter. We won't turn her out to fend for herself."

"I should hope not! I feel so sorry for her husband. Wondering where his wife is." The idea of being separated from one's family sent a cold shiver down Sabrina's spine.

"No one lives in a vacuum, Bree," he said kindly. "Think positively. Someone's sure to notice our Jane Doe didn't come home when she was supposed to and he'll report it."

"I hope you're right," she said fervently, disturbingly aware that if this situation had happened to her, it would take a while for anyone to notice and sound an alarm. More importantly, what would happen to Jeremy? She hadn't recorded a name in the "next-of-kin" box on her employment form. Neither would Jeremy's birth certificate give any clues because she'd left the space for the father's name blank, too.

"This case really bothers you, doesn't it?" he asked, uncannily accurate.

Sabrina shrugged. "I can normally be objective, but this time…I feel so sorry for her and her family. She's a lost soul and I can't imagine what her husband must be going through."

"You always cared about your patients more than most," he said. "Are you sure that's all it is?"

She refused to admit that this scenario had awakened fears that she hadn't considered—fears that should be addressed relatively soon to ensure Jeremy wouldn't be left in legal limbo. While she didn't look for tragedy at every turn, it was an equal opportunity event—no one, no matter how careful he or she was, was safe from misfortune.

Explaining that, however, would only make her appear paranoid. As thoughtful and considerate as Adrian had been these past few days, she wouldn't show any weakness that he could exploit. She'd experienced firsthand how quickly he could turn on her, so trusting him was too risky.

She drew a bracing breath. "It is. You know me," she said lightly. "I always get too wrapped up in my patients' problems, but you're right. We have to be positive and I need to stop imagining the worst-case scenario."

"I can help you with that," he said. "Let's take Jeremy to the park tonight. He wants to have a picnic."

She grinned at his matter-of-fact revelation. "Oh, he does, does he? I suppose you have a special skill and insight that allows you to understand baby-speak?"

"I do," Adrian said self-importantly. "I asked him if he wanted a trip to the park and he jabbered at me for a full five minutes. The translation definitely involved a trip to the park."

His good humor was infectious. "Really."

"Yeah. He also said that his mommy wouldn't want to go, but I should persuade her because she needs the fresh air. So, how about it? We both clock out at six. I can pick you up at half past and we'll be on our way."

Relaxing in the shady confines of the park after being cooped inside all day sounded heavenly, but spending evening after evening with Adrian wasn't wise. He'd wiggle his way into her life and then leave a gaping hole when he left.

Yet what choice did she have? She understood his need to spend time with his son. After being away from Jeremy all day, she treasured their evening hours before he fell asleep and the day's routine of work and day care repeated itself.

She had one problem. More than one, actually, but the two were intertwined. "Without going to the grocery store first, I don't have anything for a picnic."

"All right. We'll spend this evening at the grocery story and save our picnic for Friday."

"It doesn't take an entire evening to go shopping," she pointed out.

"Maybe not for groceries, but there are other things I want to shop for," he said firmly.

"Then you don't need us along. I've learned that shopping with Jeremy is an exercise in patience."

"Yes, but that was when you went alone. You aren't alone any more."

But for how long? she silently wondered.

CHAPTER FIVE

ADRIAN bounded up the sidewalk to Sabrina's door some thirty minutes after he'd left the ER at six, grinning like a loon with excitement. Granted, a shopping expedition wasn't normally something he enjoyed, but he planned to accomplish two objectives in one swoop.

Naturally, he also hoped for the perfect opportunity to kiss her again. Oh, he remembered what she'd said—no more kissing—but after their first experience, it was the only thing he could think about. Tasting her, feeling her body against his, only whetted his appetite for more of the same.

It was amazing how quickly he'd fallen into his old habit of wanting her so badly he ached. He'd only been deluding himself when he'd thought they could work together in the same facility on a platonic basis. They'd always been fuel to each other's fires and limiting their contact to the hours of their shifts wouldn't have changed that.

If not for Jeremy, though, he'd be in a position of only looking and never touching because he wouldn't have been able to convince Sabrina to see him once her shift ended. While he had to proceed slowly and tread softly, now he had unlimited possibilities to remind her of how good they'd been together.

In the back of his mind a little voice taunted him. *An honorable man would respect her wish for you to stay away.*

An honorable man probably would, he privately agreed, but being honorable had provided cold comfort on those days and nights when he'd been alone. Being honorable had cost him a great deal more than he was willing to pay. Being honorable had turned him into a bitter, frustrated man and he wanted to regain his old self. The only way to do that was to coax Sabrina back into his life.

He knocked. At the answering reply of "It's open," he strode in and found Sabrina feeding Jeremy something yellow. From the frowns on the baby's face, he clearly didn't approve of what his mother was shoveling into his mouth as fast as he spit it out.

"What *is* that?" he asked as he approached to tug on Jeremy's socked foot.

The little boy smiled, kicked and waved his arms as if happy to see him, and Adrian's heart flip-flopped with love.

"Squash."

He grimaced. "I don't blame him. By the way, do you always leave the door unlocked?"

"No, I don't, but I knew you were coming. Besides, any self-respecting thief wouldn't waste his time barging in here. I don't own anything that's worth money on the street, unless they're looking for a baby stroller."

Her answer had pacified him, but her reasons had not. "You're assuming everyone who breaks in is a thief. Any pretty single woman living alone needs to be concerned about her personal security. Our Jane Doe should have convinced you of that."

"I'm fine, Adrian. As I said, the door is usually locked."

"Good," he said, recognizing the mulish set to her jaw as a sign to drop the subject, and he did. "Do we need to make a list for the store?"

"We're only getting picnic food," she said, "not stocking the *Queen Mary*."

"No, but I noticed yesterday that your fridge was quite bare."

She shrugged. "One person doesn't eat that much."

He pressed on, determined to get answers. "I recall a time when your refrigerator was full."

"It was also a time when we were together. We aren't, so I only buy half as much as I did before."

He might have believed her if she hadn't avoided his gaze and if he'd found a few of her favorite foods, but he hadn't. Instead, he'd only seen the items familiar to students who struggled to make ends meet—macaroni and cheese, instant oriental noodles, and cans of tuna.

In his mind, other observations fell into place— her lack of furniture, the absence of her prized stereo system, the tiny apartment in a not-so-good part of town. She hadn't been in these dire straits when she'd lived in Denver and worked at Mercy Memorial. Between the move here and the expense of a baby, she was clearly struggling financially.

Immediately, he felt guilty on many levels. While she might not have much in terms of possessions, one thing she had in abundance was her pride. She probably wouldn't confide in him but he had to try.

"You have a cash-flow problem," he stated.

"What makes you say that?" Once again, she concentrated on Jeremy as if to avoid his gaze.

"The signs are here," he said bluntly. "It took me a while to put them together, but I'm right, aren't I?"

"We have everything we need, Adrian." This time she met his gaze and glared at him. "Don't imagine or imply that we don't."

"But you're doing without a lot of things."

"We have everything we need," she repeated firmly. "As for doing without, so what if we are? What I do isn't any of your business."

"If it concerns Jeremy, it concerns me."

"It doesn't concern Jeremy," she insisted.

"Tell me what I want to know or I'll ask other people my questions," he warned. "And I don't think you'd want that."

"Oh, all right," she groused, clearly irritated by his persistence. "Yes, money is tight. I ended up with a few more expenses than I'd anticipated, but I'm making headway in my debts."

"How?"

"Whatever you do, Adrian, do *not* offer money because I won't take it. I don't want anything from you. I won't be a charity case again."

He paused, surprised by her vehemence. "Is it that distasteful to accept a helping hand?"

She scoffed. "Absolutely. You pay for your so-called helping hand one way or another. Nothing is ever free."

"I wouldn't ask you to pay."

"Sometimes you pay with something more precious than money. You pay with a part of yourself. When I was growing up I wore my cousins' hand-me-downs because my aunt refused to spend money on new clothes for me. I was told to be grateful.

"I took a paper route so I could have money to buy what the other girls took for granted. I'll never forget the time I stood in the checkout lane and discovered I was a quarter short and had to choose which item I wouldn't buy while people waited impatiently in line for me to finish. A generous soul took pity on me and made up the difference. I was grateful, but had never been so embarrassed."

Now he understand where her strong sense of pride had been born. "OK, if you won't accept a gift, how about a loan?"

"I have all the loans I need. Save your money for Clay…or your redheaded girlfriend. How is she handling your separation these days?"

"I don't know. But as you've mentioned her, I spent last night thinking of all the women I know who fit your description. The only one I can recall was Clay's physical therapist."

"That must have been convenient for you."

Inwardly, he smiled at her sarcasm because he wanted to believe it implied she still cared, even if it was only subconsciously. "Actually, she never came to the house. In fact, once I thought of her, I remembered the day you saw us together. She'd just come from Clay's room to tell me that he could feel his toes. It was quite an emotional moment for all of us."

The anger on her face turned to surprised dismay. "Oh."

"It certainly makes me wonder how differently our lives would have turned out if you two had had better timing," he mused aloud.

"We'll never know, will we?" She took Jeremy out of his carrier. "I'll change his diaper and then we can go."

Adrian knew if he wanted to provide any sort of financial assistance, he'd have to be creative. And he was.

By the time they'd reached the checkout counter at the grocery store, he'd filled the cart to the heaped stage.

"We can't possibly take all this to our picnic tomorrow," she complained. "Apples *and* oranges? Three kinds of cheese. Two pounds of ham and turkey. And all your fresh vegetables will spoil before they're eaten. Unless you plan to invite the entire ER staff to join us."

"Then we'll both be able to pack our lunches," he said, unconcerned.

She tried to separate the package of disposable diapers and the cans of formula away from his items, but he stopped her. "Leave them," he ordered.

"I can pay for Jeremy's things," she protested.

"I'm sure you can," he said smoothly, "but consider this a belated baby-shower present."

"That isn't necessary."

"No, it isn't, but unless you want to make a scene, I'd suggest you simply smile and say 'Thank you'."

For a moment he thought she'd argue. She'd squared her shoulders and looked ready to scold him, but then, as if she realized the futility, her stance relaxed and she offered a resigned half-smile. "Thanks."

The next day, as soon as Sabrina stepped out to take a well-deserved fifteen-minute break, Adrian cornered Hilary. "I saw Sabrina again last night," he commented.

"Again? I thought you two weren't going out at all until Friday?"

He flashed her a sheepish grin. "I jumped the gun. I couldn't wait."

She frowned at him. "As much as I'd like to see Sabrina with someone who'll appreciate her, with all due respect, you're one of those here-today-gone-tomorrow fellas. She doesn't need someone who'll cut out on her just when she's starting to depend on him."

"No, she doesn't," he agreed.

"Long-distance relationships usually don't work out, either."

"Ours will."

"You sound awfully certain."

He was, but of all the things he and Sabrina had discussed, announcing to the world that he was Jeremy's father hadn't been one of them. Once word leaked out—and it would, either by choice or by accident—the staff would treat him differently because their loyalties lay with Sabrina. After enjoying a more congenial work atmosphere and being treated like one of the guys, he selfishly didn't want to ruin a good thing until he proved himself to Sabrina and every one else.

He shrugged. "I have a gut feeling."

"Hmmm. Time will tell," she said ominously before she changed the subject. "What do you think of her little boy?"

"He's great," Adrian said, warming to the subject just as Sabrina always did. "He's so much fun to be around and he does the most interesting things for a baby his age. I've not seen a kid so inquisitive. Why, just last night, he jabbered for so long and was so serious about the noises he was making, it was like having a conversation. And he's so determined to start crawling." He grinned, remembering how Jeremy had maneuvered himself to his hands and knees before looking at Adrian as if to ask, What comes next?

He felt Hilary's careful study, her black-eyed gaze sharp, and hoped he hadn't blown his cover by sounding more like a proud papa than Bree's prospective suitor. "What can I say?" He shrugged. "I like kids."

"You know," she mused aloud, "a lot of men would consider that child as baggage or a necessary evil to get to his mama."

"They would," he agreed, "but I'm not one of them."

"Hmmm." The speculation in her eyes suddenly took on a knowing gleam. "You're his daddy, aren't you?" she asked in her southern drawl.

Startled by her insight as well as her daring, he struggled to frame an answer.

"By the way you're flapping your jaw, I'd say so," the charge nurse decided. She crossed her arms and a mulish expression appeared on her pudgy features. "If you ask me, that girl is far too forgiving, especially after everything she's handled by herself."

"We had a falling out," he said stiffly, "and I didn't know she was pregnant when she left. I'm not proud of the way she had to handle things on her own, but she won't go it alone from now on."

He felt Hilary's gaze as if she was trying to determine his sincerity, then she nodded.

"Good."

"The problem is, I know she's having financial difficulties, but she won't be specific—at least, not to me. Which is why I've come to you for answers."

Sabrina's reasons involved more than pride, he decided. A year's worth of mistrust tagged along, too. He hadn't helped matters either when he'd hinted at pursuing legal action by his fathers-have-rights-too comment. No doubt she was afraid that his more secure financial position would give him an edge with the courts.

So much for hoping she'd tell him about her troubles herself.

"If she won't talk, then I shouldn't, either. Every woman is entitled to her secrets."

"I'm not asking for her account numbers or her bank balance," he said sharply. "Why don't I tell you what I think and you can tell me if I'm right or wrong?"

Hilary pinched her bottom lip in obvious indecision. "This is against my better judgement," she finally said, "but if you're that boy's daddy, you should know the facts. Just remember, though. You didn't hear this from me."

He pantomimed locking his mouth. "My lips are sealed."

Thinking of the photo he'd seen in her album, he began. "She probably had a rough pregnancy and missed a lot of work."

Hilary clutched the clipboard to her chest. "That isn't the half of it. At first she just had morning sickness, but it lasted all day. There were times I found her retching in the bathroom between patients. In fact, sometimes I thought she was sicker than most of the folks who came in by ambulance. The doctor wanted to admit her, but she refused. She finally agreed to cut her hours to part time and sold a lot of her furniture to make ends meet.

"After that stage finally passed, her blood pressure went haywire. This time she gave in when the doctor told her to stop working because, as she told me, she couldn't afford to lose her baby."

He was all I had. Hilary's words twisted the knife that Sabrina had thrust into his gut. "So Sabrina spent the final months of her pregnancy at home and probably took out a loan for her living expenses," he guessed.

Hilary's nod confirmed his theory.

"But that doesn't explain why she's still broke. Doesn't Pinehaven pay for the employees' single coverage health insurance policies?"

"They do," Hilary agreed, "except for maternity benefits within one year of enrollment in the plan."

That explained it. The situation was worse than he'd thought. A high-interest loan for living expenses, a huge hospital and doctor's bill, as well as expenses associated with a baby meant Sabrina had to stretch her dollar beyond the breaking point. Considering he was responsible for her circumstances, he was surprised Sabrina spoke to him at all.

"So," Hilary said after a soft sigh, "she picks up extra shifts whenever she can."

"How often?"

"Once, sometimes twice a week. In fact, she shouldn't be here today, but one of the nurses wanted to attend her niece's wedding, so Sabrina agreed to cover."

His head reeled from what he'd heard. No wonder she looked as if a strong wind would blow her into the next state. "I knew money was tight," he said hoarsely, "but I had no idea her finances were this bad."

"You aren't going to get all high and mighty, are you?" she asked, frowning. "Because if you do, you can forget having picnics or anything else with her. The girl doesn't have much, but she's got plenty of pride."

"More than enough," he agreed. But, pride or not, he knew his duty. It was time to take matters into his own hands and proceed with the rest of his plan.

"What are you going to do?" Hilary asked. "She has this aversion to accepting charity."

"There's more than one way to take a temperature, but it's best you don't know the details. That way, if she questions you, you can honestly tell her you don't know anything."

"Oh, good idea."

"Rest assured, her circumstances will improve."

Hilary's grin slowly grew to spread across her entire face. "This I can't wait to see."

"And you won't breathe a word about this to anyone?"

"Not one word," she agreed, "but I never would have guessed I'd run into Santa Claus in August."

Santa Claus he wasn't. Writing a check wouldn't come close to putting him in the same league as the jolly, benevolent fellow but it would serve as the first installment toward paying for his sins.

"It was a good idea to come here this evening." Sabrina sat on the blanket under the shade of the tree Adrian had chosen and stared at Jeremy, who was sitting contentedly between Adrian's spread legs, apparently fascinated by the hem of Adrian's khaki shorts.

"It was Jeremy's, not mine," he said.

If he wanted to give their son the credit, that was his prerogative. She was too relaxed to argue. "I don't care whose idea it was, it was a good one."

"I'm not so sure," he admitted, wiping the beads of perspiration off his forehead. "It's still over ninety degrees. We should either be lounging in a pool or sitting in air-conditioned comfort."

"We don't mind the heat, do we, sprout?" She leaned over and smoothed down Jeremy's wispy hair, eliciting a toothy grin. "This way, we have the park to ourselves. Right now, a pool would be too crowded for us to enjoy."

"Not true," he protested. "And the view would be great. You always did look fantastic in a swimsuit."

Her face warmed under his hungry gaze, as much a result of his compliment as her own heated thoughts. She hadn't forgotten their last trip to a pool even though it seemed like a lifetime ago. Adrian's knee-length trunks had covered a fair amount of skin, but the black Spandex had outlined well-defined quadriceps and a trim gluteus maximus to mouth-drooling, take-a-second-look perfection.

"That was before I had a baby," she said lightly, before she felt his perusal.

"Every pound you gained must have been Junior here, because it looks as if you've lost weight."

"A little," she admitted, "but keeping up with an infant and a hectic work schedule will do that."

"Hmmm," he said, sounding unconvinced. In the next instant his expression changed as he yelped.

Concern brought her to her feet as she watched him rub at a spot on his shin. "What's wrong? Was it a bee? Did you get stung? Is Jeremy—?"

"Jeremy's fine," Adrian said calmly. "He just discovered the hair on my leg."

"Oh. Is that all?" she teased, relieved there hadn't been any danger. "From the sound of your scream, I thought you were mortally wounded."

"I didn't scream. I yelped," he pointed out.

"There's a difference?" she teased.

"You bet there is. Women scream. Men yelp." Jeremy grabbed at his leg again, and Adrian grabbed his little hand and kissed it. "Our son needs a new toy. Pass his bag, will you?"

Sabrina handed the drawstring tote to him and tried not to like the sound of "our son" too much. That particular pronoun implied a connection—a bond—that went beyond the two of them physically creating a baby together.

Idly, she wondered if Jeremy himself wasn't providing the healing balm they needed to truly bury the past. Time would tell.

Adrian dug inside the bag and pulled out a set of plastic rings, but Jeremy batted them away. "OK, try this." He held out a stuffed mouse and pinched its sides until it squeaked. Again, Jeremy refused his offering.

"One more time," he said as he thrust his hand back into the bag and drew out another item. "Well, well, what do you know? My toothbrush." He studied it with a furrowed brow as if trying to figure out how this particular item had become a toy, especially a toy with deep gouges in the plastic grip. "There are tooth marks on it."

They'd been caught, her secret was out! "When I was collecting your things while you were in hospital, Jeremy wanted to hold it. By the time I got it away from him, he'd left his mark. I couldn't let you see it without explaining everything, so it became his."

"And you bought me a new one."

"Yes."

Immediately, Jeremy reached for the brush and grunted. As soon as Adrian handed it over, Jeremy began gnawing on the bright blue handle.

"I think he likes the color," she said tentatively, hoping Adrian wouldn't comment on her duplicity.

Instead he smiled. "We'll have to teach him the other end belongs in his mouth."

"You're not upset?"

"About him playing with my toothbrush? No. For you not using it as an opportunity to tell me about him? I'm more disappointed than upset, but I'll get over it."

Jeremy alternated between beating the brush against his leg like a drumstick and chewing on it as if it were a teething ring. "I'm just grateful you didn't recycle it as a toilet brush," Adrian added.

"There is that possibility," she said lightly.

"So what *do* you do on your days off?"

"Clean the house, go to the laundromat, sew, take care of Jeremy."

"I didn't hear you mention golf."

"After the way I sliced the ball the other day, isn't it rather obvious I haven't played for a long time?" she asked wryly.

"Everyone slices the ball. I'll bet Tiger Woods does every now and then, too."

She laughed. "Somehow, I doubt it, but thanks for being so forgiving. If you must know, the benefit tournament was the first time I'd set foot on the Pinehaven course. Green fees are horrific and I don't golf enough to justify paying for membership. I'd also have to pay a babysitter, which I'm not able, er, willing to do.' She hoped he hadn't noticed her slip of the tongue. It was bad enough that he knew she was having trouble making ends meet; he didn't need to know just how financially strapped she was. With information like that, it would be hard to say what a judge might decide if Adrian forced a custody issue.

"Honestly, though," she continued, "I'd rather spend my free hours with Jeremy. The hospital day care is great, but it makes his day rather long. On the other hand, working twelve-hour stretches means I usually work three days a week instead of four or five."

"Unless you fill in for someone else."

"It happens from time to time," she agreed.

His blue-eyed gaze seemed to see into her thoughts. "Hilary mentioned you tend to pick up at least one extra shift a week, sometimes two."

Surely the well-meaning nurse hadn't explained that her bills were her main reason for working those additional hours. "A lot of nurses covered for me when I was pregnant, so I reciprocate whenever I can." She raised her chin in defiance. "Jeremy doesn't suffer for it. Our hospital day care is excellent."

He raised an eyebrow. "I'm sure it is. Did I imply that he seemed deprived because he spent the day without his mother?"

"No," she said slowly, "but you'd always said…" Her voice died before she could complete her sentence.

"I always said what?"

"It doesn't matter."

"It does. I want you to finish. I'd always said what?"

"That you wanted your wife to stay at home for the kids. That you didn't want a sitter to raise them."

"What's wrong with that? If I had a wife, it would be the ideal situation, but we both know life doesn't allow for many ideal situations. Who knows?" He shrugged. "She may pursue a career instead of being a stay-at-home mom, and if that's the case, I wouldn't stand in her way. As for Jeremy, if he's at the best day care possible, I'm satisfied."

Suddenly the discussion took on an ominous tone. She didn't want to think about Adrian getting married. The notion of sending her baby for another woman to love—or possibly mistreat—sent a cold shiver down her spine. But she had to know how imminent or remote the possibility was.

"Now that I know about the woman I saw you with that time," she said lightly to hide her concern, "you've been footloose for the past year. I'm sure you've dated. Did you meet a potential candidate for a wife?"

"No," he admitted as he placed Jeremy on his tummy and shifted positions. "I've been too busy with work and Clay's therapy to see anyone. Plus, I haven't been the nicest of guys, so even if I'd wanted to go out, women have steered clear of me."

"Really? I find that hard to believe. As I recall, the nurses collectively drooled over you." At the time, she could hardly believe someone so handsome and debonair who could have had his pick of available—, and the not-so-available—women had chosen *her*. Of course, he'd eventually dropped her like a hot potato, but that was beside the point.

He smiled. "Not any more. People tend to avoid bears with sore heads."

At that moment Jeremy began to fuss, and Sabrina was grateful for the interruption. She rose and stretched out the kinks in her back. "Sounds like he's had enough of the park experience for one evening."

"Probably so."

Back at her house, Sabrina prepared Jeremy's evening snack of cereal with a dollop of strained fruit while Adrian bounced the fussy baby as they paced her tiny living room like a pair of caged tigers. "How much longer?" Adrian asked.

"It's ready now." She set the bowl on the table. "And if I remember correctly, it's your turn to feed him."

"Oh, sure," Adrian commented good-naturedly. "When he's in a grumpy mood, I get the honor."

"Hey, I'm just giving what you asked for, and that was to share the routine. Would you rather unpack and sterilize his bottles?"

He grimaced. "Pass the spoon."

So, while Adrian fed Jeremy, Sabrina took care of her tasks at the sink. As she listened to Adrian's one-sided conversation with their son and Jeremy's smacking lips, she realized how family-like this scene seemed. Mom and Dad sharing in the care of a baby. This was what she would have had from the beginning and it would be what she'd have in the years ahead if only events had tran-spired differently…

No, she told herself. Don't go there. The "what if" and "if only" paths only led to unfulfilled dreams and disappointment. But for a long moment she wished that *she* could be the recipient of Adrian's attention, that he'd come for the sole purpose to visit *her* and not Jeremy.

She was being ridiculous. Why *would* he bother? She'd already warned him away after he'd kissed her so why would he break the rules and risk not being able to see his son?

As impossible as their circumstances were, she wanted him to break the rules.

Pathetic. She was positively pathetic. In a few short months they'd go their separate ways again and she'd be left with more recent memories to haunt her.

Much later, after Jeremy had eaten, splashed in the sink, and drunk his last bottle for the evening nestled in Sabrina's lap, and after she'd carefully laid him in his crib, Adrian hesitated at the front door.

"What do you have planned tomorrow?" he asked.

"Chores, laundry. Like I told you earlier, the usual stuff."

"Do you mind if I spend the day here?"

"Do you want to?" she asked, surprised by his request.

"Spending a few hours every day with you and Jeremy isn't an obligation," he insisted. "It's something I want to do. Provided you agree."

Part of her was thrilled by his request because in these few short days she'd gotten spoiled by having him nearby. They still had unresolved issues, but they were talking like the friends they had once been instead of sparring like enemies.

It wouldn't be wise for her to fall in love with him again because it could easily happen if he continued acting like the man she'd loved nearly two years ago.

Unwilling to say yes and hating to say no, she chose her words carefully. "Are you sure you don't want a few days to yourself in an apartment that's bigger than a postage stamp? One with more comfortable furniture than a broken-down recliner?"

"We had some good times in that recliner. Not as many as on your sofa, but enough. If I stayed in my quiet apartment, what would I do all day besides read the newspaper or watch television? The only people I know in town are those I work with, you and Jeremy, and I'd rather hang around with you two."

"I assumed you'd go back to Denver on the weekends. Back to your other life." Actually, she hadn't thought that far ahead, but her idea made sense.

"I'd planned to," he confessed, "but that was before I knew about Jeremy. As for my so-called 'other' life, it's so similar to this one, it's ridiculous. I go to work and I come home, watch the news, and eat take-out. The only difference is that I don't have any home maintenance projects or yardwork here."

For a man who liked to stay busy, she understood how stressful it would be to live a life of relative leisure. However, no matter how bored he might be, regardless of how much she'd come to enjoy his company, *she* needed some distance. Being in his near-constant presence was reviving her fairy-tale imagination where the prince found his Cinderella and everyone lived happily ever after. Those fantasies simply weren't going to happen.

"In any case, I need to drive back on Sunday to pick up my mail and make new arrangements with my neighbor who's watching the house. I was hoping you and Jeremy would come along."

Logically, it wasn't a wise idea to go anywhere with Adrian. In her heart, though, she wanted it more than she should. "It isn't a good idea for us to spend so much time together," she said gently.

"Are you saying I can't see Jeremy?"

"No, I just don't think we should be together every single day."

"I'm only in town for a few months, remember? I'd like to create as many memories as I can in the short time I have."

Phrased like that, she couldn't argue with or deny his request. If the situation were reversed, she'd ask for the same consideration. However, at the same time she didn't have to ask what his future plans were. He'd stated plainly he would leave at the end of his contract period.

Surprisingly enough, the idea irritated her. How could he think it would be acceptable to breeze in, make himself indispensable for a few months, then disappear?

For that reason alone she wanted to pass the weekend like all the previous ones—just her and her son. Cooperating with him might be in her future best interests, but cooperation would also come at great emotional expense. After being around him for less than a week, she didn't know if she could guard against falling for his charm again. She was in a no-win situation.

Reluctantly and against her better judgement, she consented. "OK. We'll go with you."

His eyes lit up and a smile spread across his face. "Great. We don't have to leave too early and we'll be back in plenty of time so we won't disrupt Jeremy's bedtime schedule. Thanks, Bree."

He stepped forward and planted a firm but swift kiss on her mouth before he withdrew. "Sorry," he said, clearly unrepentant. "Don't be angry, but I couldn't help myself."

The kiss had ended before it had really begun, but it had lasted long enough to stir those unwanted and unrealistic romantic feelings. Irritated by her weakness for a man who'd once shattered her world, she simply pretended to be exasperated by his blatant disregard for their rules. "Yeah right."

"It's true," he insisted, his eyes twinkling. "Thanks for being so understanding and generous. We're going to have a wonderful weekend. Wait and see."

Understanding and generous, hah! He should have described her as a pushover—a sucker for a sad story—but it was too late to change her mind when she'd already agreed. She only hoped she wouldn't live to regret her hasty and completely irrational decision.

CHAPTER SIX

ADRIAN bounded up the walk on Sunday morning, eager for the impending trip. He'd already phoned Clay and invited him to his house that afternoon for a surprise, and he couldn't wait to see the look on his brother's face when he discovered he was an uncle!

He knocked impatiently on Sabrina's door and heard Jeremy's muted wail. Smiling at the volume, he began to worry when she didn't answer and Jeremy didn't stop crying. Taking a chance, because Sabrina knew when he'd arrive, he tried the knob and found it unlocked. Pushing his way inside, he went straight to Jeremy's playpen where he lay kicking and screaming.

"What's wrong, big fella?" he crooned as he hoisted Jeremy into his arms. "Are you hungry, wet, or just tired of being stuck in your playpen alone?"

Jeremy sniffled and bobbed his head against Adrian's shoulder.

"Sabrina?" Adrian called.

She came out of the bathroom, still wearing a short-sleeved sleep shirt that fell to mid-thigh and revealed plenty of long leg. "You're here," she said inanely as she fingercombed her hair.

"It's ten o'clock," he pointed out. "We'd planned to leave for our trip, remember?"

She visibly winced. "We can't go."

He bounced Jeremy and frowned. "Why not?"

"I'm not able to take a trip today. I'm sorry."

Disappointment sent his upbeat spirits into a downward spiral, but he suddenly noticed the dark circles under her eyes, her abnormally pale face and shaky hands. Immediately concerned, he asked, "What's wrong?"

She heaved a sigh, almost as if she hated to admit her problem. "Migraine."

He'd forgotten she suffered from those intense headaches. "When did it start?"

"Last night, after you left. I thought it would ease if I went to bed early, but it hasn't."

He'd seen her like this before. Nothing had cut the pain except medication and rest. "Did you take your pills?"

Slowly, she headed for the kitchen and he followed, watching her gingerly grab a bag of peas from the freezer and place it just as carefully on her forehead. "Well?" he demanded.

"No."

He cursed. "Why not?"

"I don't have a prescription."

"Why don't you?"

"Because it expired and I haven't asked my doctor to write another. Even if I did, I wouldn't fill it because those pills are too expensive." She repositioned the frozen peas to cover the right side of her head. "I'll be fine in a few hours."

"You and I both know an ice pack won't do the trick," he said bluntly.

"Yes, well, ice and over-the-counter pain relievers and anti-inflammatories are all I have. They worked before and they'll work again."

"On an attack this severe? How often do you get them? Are you avoiding your triggers?"

She held up one hand. "Turn down the volume, please."

Instantly contrite, he lowered his voice. "Sorry. How often are you getting these headaches?"

"Not often. Every couple of months."

"What can I do?"

"Nothing. I'm really sorry we can't go with

you, but have fun and call us when you get back into town."

Leave her like this? When she could hardly walk, much less take care of Jeremy? His trip didn't seem important right now. "You're not in any shape to look after yourself, much less a baby."

"I can handle it," she insisted. "I've done it before and I'll do it again. Don't give us another thought."

"Sorry, Bree, but there's no way I'm leaving you to manage on your own. You can hardly stand. How are you going to lift or carry him?"

"I'll call Kate if I run into a problem."

"You already had a problem," he said flatly. "How long would Jeremy have cried in his playpen if I hadn't walked in when I did?"

"Not long," she said defensively.

"Why call Kate when I'm already here?" He tried not to feel hurt by her obvious rejection. Apparently these past few days hadn't convinced her to rely on him. How ironic to realize he'd finally tasted a dose of his own medicine.

"My trip to Denver can wait for another day. You…" he grabbed her arm as much to steady her as to lead her "…are going straight to bed."

"I can't. Too many chores."

"We did everything yesterday from laundry to grocery shopping to vacuuming," he reminded her.

"I can't imagine what we left undone, but whatever it is can wait another day or two."

"Jeremy's hungry," she said.

"Then I'll feed him."

"But—"

"If you don't trust me to take care of him, then tell me how to contact Kate," he said, hoping she wouldn't.

To his great relief, she didn't. "Fine." She gave in wearily. "Go for it. But if you have a question…"

"I'll ask you," he promised.

"Emergency numbers are posted by the phone. Poison control, his pediatrician, the hospital."

He wanted to remind her of his own medical degree, then decided it was simpler and faster to listen to her spiel about where to find the teething rings, extra diapers and a spare pacifier in case the primary binky got lost—in the freezer, under the bathroom sink, and in his dresser, respectively.

While she wrapped up her instructions, he placed Jeremy in the swing contraption, wound the handle and set the seat in motion before guiding her into the bedroom. "Come on. You'll feel better after you lie down."

He'd expected more of an argument, but she obviously felt terrible because she meekly let him help her onto the mattress. An instant later, he closed the blinds against the morning sun and left the room.

"It's you and me, bud," he told Jeremy. "Hang tight and I'll be right back."

A phone call, a diaper change and a bottle of warm formula later, Jeremy was fast asleep.

Debating on whether or not to cart him along on his errand of mercy, he wondered what would be worse. Sabrina waking up and discovering Jeremy was missing, or Jeremy crying and she couldn't respond? He chose to haul the baby with him.

Just in case she did stir before he got home again, he scribbled a note and placed it in Jeremy's crib, then quietly left the house. After some struggles due to inexperience, he strapped the baby carrier in backwards as he'd seen his friends do with their children's safety seats, and carefully drove to a nearby pharmacy.

By the time he returned, both mother and baby were still asleep. He opted to address Sabrina's needs first.

"Sabrina," he said softly, as he shook one large, white tablet out of the prescription bottle, "swallow this."

She opened bleary eyes. "What is it?"

"Your migraine pill."

"How…? Where…?"

"Don't ask questions, just sit up and swallow."

As soon as she'd downed the medicine, along with a liberal amount of water, she sank back onto her pillow. "Thanks," she mumbled, closing her eyes.

Suddenly hesitant to leave, he watched her and noticed the lines of strain around her eyes and mouth. In days past she would have welcomed one of his head and neck massages until the pill took the edge off her pain. Now she wouldn't appreciate his efforts.

As he settled Jeremy in his crib, he heard her whimper in her sleep. *Oh, what the hell*, he thought. She might not want his non-traditional therapy, but he had to do more than twiddle his thumbs and watch her suffer.

He perched on the edge of the bed, touched her temples with a feather-light caress, then began his gentle massage. If she only took her over-the-counter meds every few months instead of two or three times a week, then she wasn't setting herself up for a complication known as "rebound" head-aches—a condition when the treatment actually caused the headache instead of relieving it.

As he ran through his med-school lecture by a neurologist on this very subject, he remembered how migraines loved change. Any variations in one's life, whether it involved a disruption in the sleep cycle, missed meals or being exposed to sudden stress, could easily act as the trigger.

From what he'd seen during the past week, any one or all of those things could be the culprit. Babies weren't known to have regular sleeping habits; Sabrina obviously didn't eat properly or regularly; and his appearance in her life had clearly raised her stress level.

With painstaking care, he gradually smoothed away the tension with slow, soothing strokes. By the time the furrows between her brows became less pronounced, he began noticing as well as remembering other things—like how soft her skin felt. How her hair smelled like spring flowers. How it felt to have her long legs wrapped around him. How the curve of her breasts beckoned for his hands...

He wanted her badly, but he didn't feel worthy of this woman. He'd failed her in so many ways and he considered himself lucky that he'd wriggled his way this far into her good graces. Unfortunately, he still wasn't to the point where she willingly depended on him. The only reason he was sitting beside her now was because she'd been too wiped out from the pain to protest.

He wanted to be her first choice, not the consolation prize. Dammit, he *wanted* to be here with her and their son twenty-four seven, not just for a few hours every evening. He wanted to watch Jeremy take his first steps, to hear his first recognizable words, to teach him new things and see his wide-eyed wonderment. He wanted to give Jeremy a brother or a sister.

Family meant everything to him. It always had and always would. His father had passed his responsibility for his children to Adrian and he'd willingly accepted them. Now he wanted to accept one more. Regardless of the details surrounding Jeremy's conception, that small child was *his* to nurture and to take care of. He simply had to figure out a way to juggle both sets of commitments in two different locations.

He leaned over and brushed his mouth against hers. "We *will* work something out, Bree," he whispered. "Count on it."

To his surprise, she murmured, "I waited for you…but you took so long. So very long…"

It had only been twelve hours since he'd last seen her and she considered that to be a long time? She could have called him and he would have broken speed records to drive across town, until he realized he'd never given her his cellphone number and she'd never asked.

"I'm here now, Bree," he said instead.

Her hand moved to her abdomen. "Can you feel our baby kicking? Do you want a boy or a girl?"

In that instant, he realized she was caught up in a state where dreams and memories intermingled and she was talking in her sleep.

"I don't care," he said hoarsely, "as long as it's healthy."

"Me, too." She sighed. "I'm so tired."

"Then sleep."

"You'll stay? Beside me?"

He hesitated, knowing how tough it would be to lie next to her without driving himself utterly crazy, but there was no other place he'd rather be at this particular moment.

"I'll stay." Carefully, he got in to bed from the other side, then pulled her against him.

"Love you," she mumbled.

The words caught him by surprise before he decided she had to be dreaming. He may have made progress in paying for his sins, but she was still too wary to hand her heart over to him so easily.

She would, though. He'd failed at other things in his life, but he wouldn't at this one.

* * *

Sabrina slowly drifted awake with the most wonderful sense of well-being. It was unbelievable because normally, when the migraine pain faded, she woke up feeling exhausted. She grabbed her watch off the bedside table and read the display. Twelve-fifteen.

How could she feel this good after a two-hour nap? But it had to be, because the sun was shining. She couldn't have slept for twenty-four hours, but as she glanced at the date on her watch face, she realized it was true. A full day had passed.

Jeremy! Dear heavens, who'd taken care of him if she'd slept that long?

Fear speared her chest as she took in the empty bed and she bolted upright. The diaper bag was missing, too. Ready to call 911 and report a child abduction, she noticed a piece of paper taped to the crib's headboard.

The note was in Adrian's handwriting.

She snatched it free and scanned it. *Dear Bree*, it began.

Don't worry about Jeremy. I took him to the hospital day care. He'll be there, waiting for you to pick him up, but if you don't find this before I get off duty, I'll bring him by on my way home. Adrian.

P.s. You're officially on a sick day today. Hilary says to take care of yourself.

Relieved Jeremy was in a safe place, she was also furious with Adrian's presumptuous decision to report her as sick. He didn't have the right!

Common sense, however, said she was fighting a foolish battle. Those extra hours of uninterrupted sleep had been exactly what she'd needed; on previous occasions, she'd carried on as usual and had felt drained for days. Instead of finding fault, she should thank him from the bottom of her heart.

She sank onto the edge of the bed and tried to recall the previous day, but only bits and pieces came to mind. Adrian had come by for their trip, but she'd sent him away. He couldn't have gone to Denver, because he'd always seemed to be waking her to take a pill or to drink something. Which reminded her…she'd have to reimburse him for her prescription.

At one point, she was certain he'd kissed her, because she'd imagined the feel of his lips on hers, but that had surely been a dream, hadn't it?

She'd also felt cozy and secure, almost as if he'd held her, but either her subconscious had worked overtime or she'd dredged up ancient memories. Yet, as she gazed at the pillow beside hers and noticed a faint indentation as if someone's head had rested there, she came to an undeniable conclusion.

Adrian had spent the night there. He hadn't just spent the night, either. He'd *slept* with her, in her room, in her bed.

Oh, my. No wonder she'd felt so warm and cozy. She'd always gravitated to his warmth because she was usually cold, so she had probably used him as her pillow and blanket. For a woman who'd tried to maintain emotional distance, how would she face him?

There was nothing *to* face, she scolded herself. She'd practically been unconscious, and if she'd made any inappropriate overtures, Adrian would chalk them up to her being out of her mind with pain. He wouldn't have taken advantage of her, because at heart he *was* an honorable man.

As she gazed at Jeremy's crib, she couldn't quite decide if she should feel grateful for Adrian's help or not. The truth of the matter was that she'd tried calling Kate as soon as she'd noticed the blind spots in her vision some thirty minutes before the pain had hit, but Kate hadn't answered. While she'd battled with her pride about contacting Adrian because she hated to give him any reason to doubt her ability to take care of Jeremy, her migraine struck full force. In the end, she'd had to rely on him.

That wasn't quite true. She hadn't *had* to do anything. She could have insisted that he track down Kate. Even though he wouldn't have wanted to, he would have because she'd asked.

She wasn't reluctant to trust him with Jeremy; even in the middle of her migraine attack, she'd known her son had been safe with him. What wasn't safe, though, was her heart because much as it pained her to admit it, she was falling in love with him all over again. And that fact made it far too easy to pretend they were a happy family.

The problem was, she *shouldn't* love him. She did once, and look where it had gotten her. Starting over in a new community with a new job, pregnant, all sorts of expenses. In her opinion, it was far too dangerous, not to mention horribly one-sided to love him again when Jeremy was the only glue holding them together. She simply had to rein in her wishful thinking. Maybe she could reluctantly accept that his motives had been altruistic and he'd only been trying to spare her, but what would happen the next time?

OK, so she knew he took his familial respon-sibilities seriously and probably wouldn't repeat his past mistake, but it was all about Jeremy. No matter what happened and to whom, he'd never push Jeremy away because he wanted him in his life in the worst way. To Adrian, she would simply be the means to his end because to get to Jeremy, he had to go through her first.

How pitiful for her to be jealous of her own son!

But thinking of her energetic baby with his ready smile and sweet temperament made her realize how badly she wanted him in her arms, at home. If she had gotten an extra day off, she intended to spend as much of it as possible with the little boy who was her entire life.

Adrian had never considered himself a clock-watcher, but he did today. He'd wanted to call Sabrina to see how she was doing, but if she was sleeping—and he hoped she was—he didn't want to wake her. He also hoped that his efforts yesterday would finally break through their relationship stalemate.

The sudden appearance of a tall fellow with a haggard expression on his face interrupted his thoughts. "I'm Dr Malloy. Thomas Malloy. I understand you treated a Jane Doe last week?"

"Yes, I did. How can I help you?"

"I'm her husband. May we talk privately?"

"Sure." Adrian led him to the small medical staff office and closed the door. "I probably can't tell you much because of the privacy acts."

"I know. I've already spoken to the police and they told me everything. What I'd like to know is your impression of her mental state."

"Her amnesia," Adrian guessed.

"Yes."

"Her neurologist and psychiatrist could give you more information than I can," he began.

"Probably, if I could reach them," Thomas said impatiently. "According to their secretaries, both are tied up until late this afternoon. I'd like to know something *now*."

Adrian understood the man's frustration. "Have you seen your wife yet?"

Thomas shook his head. "I was out of town at a conference when I got the news my wife was missing. You see, before I left, Abigail told me she was seeing an attorney and wanted to file for a divorce. She asked me to cancel my trip so we could talk but as one of the conference organizers, I couldn't. So…" He sighed heavily. "She arranged to visit a friend in Breckenridge while I was gone. Supposedly to think.

"Unfortunately," Thomas continued, "she hadn't confirmed her plans with her old roommate, so when Abby didn't arrive, Rosie just thought she'd changed her mind and didn't question her absence until Abby's mother called because she hadn't been able to reach her. We started searching and found her here." He paused. "When I think of what that bastard did…what happened to her…." His voice broke. "Part of me is glad she forgot all that and part of me wants her to remember this guy so he can pay."

Adrian felt for the man's pain. "I understand, but if it's any consolation, when she was in our ED, she seemed to be handling herself well. She was scared because she couldn't remember the details of her life that we take for granted, but she was calm and in relatively good health. I haven't seen her since we transferred her upstairs, so she may have regained some of her memory."

"According to the detective, she hasn't." He ran his hands through his hair. "The question is, if she wanted a divorce, do I let her go through with it, even though she can't remember?"

Adrian hesitated. He was the last person on earth to ask for marital advice. "I'm not the best person to advise you," he began. "I'm not—"

"I'm not asking for a medical opinion. I guess I'm just thinking out loud, one man to another."

Although Adrian didn't know this man, he couldn't turn his back on a fellow physician. If Malloy wanted a sounding board, Adrian would oblige. "What do *you* want to do?"

"I don't want her to leave," he said hoarsely. "The police told me we have a baby coming—our first—so I'll do whatever it takes to convince her to change her mind. I'll cut my hours, spend more time with her and the baby when it arrives, whatever. I want a second chance."

Although his own situation wasn't as dramatic as Thomas Malloy's, Adrian knew exactly how the man felt. "If that's what you want, then you should take it."

Thomas nodded. "I almost feel guilty, as if I'm tricking her, but her amnesia gives us a clean slate. We can write an entirely new future for our marriage on it."

"And if she ever does remember?" Adrian hated playing the devil's advocate, but the man needed to think of every angle.

"By then, I hope we'll have restored enough of our relationship to make her wonder why she wanted a divorce in the first place."

Adrian held out his hand. "Good luck, then. Let me know how everything turns out."

"Thanks," Thomas said, shaking Adrian's hand with a firm grip. "I will."

For the rest of the morning, Malloy's words echoed in Adrian's head. *You have a clean slate. A clean slate. A clean slate.* Several patients later, he decided to take Malloy's comment to heart.

After lunch, and after he'd explained to Maria Rios that her blood pressure was still too high and she needed to stay until they saw a response to her hypertension medication, he opened the exam-room door and heard a familiar baby laugh.

Immediately he smiled and strode toward the nurses' station, marveling at how quickly he'd learned to recognize his son's voice. "Someone's happy," he remarked as he came up to the staff gathered there.

"He loves the attention," Sabrina said, looking like a completely different woman from the one he'd seen yesterday. From the glow on her face, no one would ever know she'd suffered a debilitating migraine twenty-four hours ago.

"A typical male response when surrounded by adoring women," he said as he tugged on one of Jeremy's socked feet, eliciting another giggle and a fair amount of joyful kicking. "Lucky fellow."

"I'll say." Hilary smiled fondly at Jeremy. "Makes me eager for grandkids. Until then, I'll just have to spoil this one." She addressed Adrian. "Is Mrs Rios ready to go home?"

"Not until her blood pressure comes down. I want it taken every fifteen minutes. Call me as soon as there's a change."

"Will do." Hilary snapped her fingers at the staff still hovering around the desk. "Come on, people, back to work."

The group scattered, leaving Adrian and Sabrina behind. "I see you stopped at day care. I hope I sent enough stuff with him."

"You did. I just stopped by to let you know you didn't have to bring him home."

"I wouldn't have minded."

"Now you don't need to. Anyway, I just wanted to say thanks, for yesterday. For everything."

"You're welcome. It was my pleasure."

"You should have woke me this morning, though. I could have managed Jeremy myself."

Sensing she was trying to prove a point, he simply nodded. "Probably, but I'd say those few extra hours of sleep made a difference."

"I appreciate it, but I'm sorry you missed your trip on my account."

"I took care of nearly everything by phone. Clay's coming by tonight with my mail and to have dinner with us, so no harm done."

"Dinner? With us?"

"Yeah. I invited him to your place so I hope you don't mind, but it seemed easier for Jeremy's schedule if we spent the evening there rather than at my apartment. By the way, did you notice the steaks in your refrigerator?"

She shook her head. "No. But, Adrian," she protested, "I don't have a grill and—"

"Not to worry. Harvey's Hardware will deliver one this afternoon."

Her gaze narrowed. "What happens to the grill when you leave? I can't keep—"

"You'll use it and if you don't want the hassle when you're alone, I'll fire it up when I visit on the weekends. Remember?" He grabbed the handle on Jeremy's carrier and lifted him off the counter. "I hate to run, but if I don't get back to work, Hilary will scold me. I've learned it's not a good thing to land on the head nurse's bad side. So, I'll see you both tonight."

He strolled away, laughing inside at how he'd left Sabrina speechless. He'd enjoy his small victory while he could because when he arrived at her house tonight, the tables would be turned and he wouldn't get a word in edgewise.

CHAPTER SEVEN

"THANKS for the nice evening," Clay told Sabrina as he prepared to leave. "I had a great time meeting my nephew. I hope we can do this again."

"Absolutely," she said as she matched his uneven gait down the sidewalk while Adrian remained inside to give Jeremy his last bottle for the night. "You're welcome to drop by whenever you're in town."

"Thanks." He paused before he slid inside his blue Ford Mustang. "For what it's worth, I hope you two get back together."

She'd like that too, but only for the right reasons. "It's hard to say what will happen," she prevaricated. "Too many roadblocks are in the way." She didn't feel inclined to say that beyond the obvious issue of the physical distance between them, the biggest speed bump on her highway to happiness would be his motive.

"Road blocks are usually temporary and can be moved," he reminded her.

She laughed at his hopeful tone. "True, but it's dangerous to move them if the hazard is still on the other side."

He met her gaze calmly. "A preacher once told me that love covers a multitude of sins. Do you love him?"

Heaven help her, but she did. Every kind thing he'd done in the past week had built on the one before, but his selfless act on Sunday had turned the tide in his favor. The only problem was, he only did those kind things out of concern for Jeremy's welfare, not because he wanted to do them for *her*.

"My feelings aren't the issue," she countered as she met Clay's gaze. "Adrian's interest lies solely with Jeremy. As you know, he's fanatical about meeting his responsibilities. Right now, every choice he makes is with him in mind."

"If you say so," he said dubiously, "but I think you're wrong."

"We'll see," she said as she hugged him goodbye to purposely end the conversation. "Drive carefully and don't be a stranger. Jeremy wants to spend time with his favorite uncle."

She waited until Clay drove off before she went

inside to find Adrian coming out of her bedroom. Funny, how it seemed so natural for him to have full rein of her whole house. What would it be like when he wasn't there? She didn't want to think of how empty the place would seem.

"He's asleep so soon?" she asked.

"He's had a busy day. I presume Clay's on his way home?"

"Yeah. I was glad to see him."

"Me, too. Did you think he looked OK?"

"I haven't seen him in over a year," she reminded him. "And he doesn't look anything like he did when I saw him in hospital. Why do you ask?"

"I thought he seemed a bit pale. He didn't have much of an appetite, either."

"He polished off a salad, a large steak and a baked potato. If that wasn't much of an appetite, then I'd hate to feed him when he has one."

"You're right. It's my imagination. By the way, I found out who our Jane Doe is. Her husband stopped by to see me today."

"Really? Who is she?"

"Abigail Malloy. Before her attack, she'd apparently told her husband she was going to file for a divorce. Now that she doesn't remember, Thomas intends to fight for his marriage."

"Oh?"

"Abby's amnesia gave him a clean slate and he wants to take advantage of it. Time will tell if he's successful."

"Or if his plan backfires when she remembers."

"That, too. With any luck, when that day comes, Thomas will have shown her he's not such a bad guy after all." He hesitated. "OK, let's have it."

"Have what?"

"The tongue-lashing you've been dying to give me all evening."

She sank onto the brand-new sofa that had arrived at four o'clock, right before the hardware store had delivered the gas grill. "Patience is a virtue. Besides, knowing you're waiting for the bomb to fall is half the fun."

"Gee, thanks," he said wryly as he sat on the other end of the sofa. "I think I'd rather hear you yelling."

"I do not yell," she said loftily.

"Point taken, but you have to admit you weren't very happy with me when I got home tonight."

And she'd thought she'd hidden her feelings so well. "I wasn't."

"I assume you didn't like Jeremy's gifts."

"I completely understand why you bought presents for him. What boy wouldn't want a play golf set, a baseball mitt or a tricycle? Those were thoughtful things and I certainly wouldn't deny him a single one, even if they are several years ahead of their time."

"It never hurts to be prepared. If you don't care about Jeremy's toys, what's the problem?"

She stared at him, incredulous. "The problem is the *other* stuff. The stuff you had delivered," she reminded him.

"You didn't like the grill? I bought it because it was a lot like your old one. The one you don't own any more."

She paused, surprised he'd noticed. "It's very nice and I love it, but…"

"But what?"

"You can't buy expensive things like that."

"Would it help if I told you I'd purchased it for Jeremy?"

She raised an eyebrow. "No."

"I did," he insisted. "He has to eat and you've always liked to cook outdoors, so it seemed logical to buy something you can use on his behalf."

"Aren't you stretching your justification a bit? It will be a while before he can sink his teeth into a steak."

"Maybe so, but the point is he'll benefit in the long run."

"How do you justify the television?"

"Cartoons," he said promptly. "You don't want our child to be the only one who hasn't seen or heard of *Sesame Street*, *Dora the Explorer*, or whatever the latest kid show is, do you?"

She folded her arms. "Then explain your rationale for this sofa. I suppose you thought Jeremy needed it, too."

His smile was boyishly handsome. "He does. On rainy days, we'd pull off the sofa cushions and build forts and rafts and all kinds of things. They're also perfect for protecting furniture from suction-cup darts, woofle balls and every other projectile a boy can shoot out of a toy gun."

"You obviously gave your purchases a great deal of thought."

"I did."

"Did you give any thought as to how *I'd* feel when these things arrived? Did you consider how your gesture looks from my point of view? Aren't my household furnishings meeting your exalted standards? Or maybe you think I'm not a good provider? Because that's exactly how your so-called gifts make me feel, Adrian."

He looked horrified. "I didn't intend to question your ability to provide. I bought those things strictly because they were things you could use, although I did have a few selfish motives."

"Oh, really? What were they?"

"For one, I like to watch the evening news and I can't."

"You can always go to your apartment."

"And miss being with Jeremy? Not a chance. As for the couch, I've spent a lot of time here and will spend more in the future. In case you haven't noticed, your chairs aren't the most comfortable in the world," he said wryly.

"OK, they're not, but you can't decide what I need, Adrian, then deliver it without giving me an option or the opportunity for discussion. That's what got us into this mess in the first place!"

He raised an eyebrow. "Would you have gone shopping with me if you'd known what I wanted to buy?"

"No."

He looked smug. "I rest my case."

"OK, so I would have refused," she admitted, stroking the soft fabric with one hand, "but don't you see, Adrian? I can't accept your gifts."

"Why not?"

"Because I don't feel comfortable accepting them," she said firmly. "I can't explain it, but it doesn't feel right." She ran her palm over a cushion and marveled at the fabric's softness. "Even if it did, though, as much as I love this sofa and can use the extra seating, it's far too big."

He glanced around the room. "It does cover a lot of floor space. Poor Jeremy won't be able to crawl far, will he?"

"Not without bumping into something," she agreed. "Next, you'll want to move us to a larger apartment."

She'd spoken facetiously, but to her dismay his guilty expression spoke volumes. "Please tell me you didn't sign a lease for a new apartment."

"I didn't," he replied defensively. "I've been considering it, though."

"Adrian, so help me…" she warned.

"Now, Bree, calm down. Give me an ounce of credit, would you? I intended for the three of us to hunt for a house or an apartment together."

"I don't want to move," she insisted. Actually, she did, but she couldn't afford to.

"I'm only thinking about the future," he countered. "Jeremy will eventually need his own bedroom for privacy and for little-boy sleepovers. But even before then, I'll be visiting on a regular basis. As much as I'm willing to do whatever it takes to spend time with Jeremy, I'm past the age when spending the night on the cold, hard floor is fun."

Obviously, the future he had in mind was for her to provide him with what basically amounted to a home away from home. If he actually paid for the apartment, it would only worsen the situation. She might as well stamp "mistress" on her forehead, she thought in disgust.

"The floor wouldn't be so terrible," she countered. "You two could use sleeping bags. It would be your weekend adventure."

"Adventure is right. An adventure in pain."

"If the floor isn't an option, you can always have the sofa." She patted the cushion beside her. "Or stay in a real hotel."

He looked thoughtful. "You're right. Jeremy and I could camp out in luxury. Between the indoor pool, room service and the on-site restaurant, we wouldn't have to leave the building the entire time I'm in town."

The thought of being excluded didn't sit well in her chest. She'd like to think they were years away from that scenario, but she knew of one divorced couple who shuttled their two-year-old from his mother's house during the week to his father's on the weekend. Her stomach churned just thinking about it.

"On the other hand," he continued, "if you consider my original plan, which gave you a large enough place for all of us, when Jeremy and I did our guy things together, he'd still be at home and I wouldn't disrupt your routine. You'd hardly know I was there."

Oh, she'd know if he was there or not. In the short time he'd been visiting, he'd created such a presence in her house that it seemed remarkably empty whenever he was gone. For a woman who was used to being alone, she was amazed at how easily she'd grown to enjoy having him around.

As for her routine, Adrian may have slipped into their lives without causing a ripple, but he'd certainly disrupted her peace of mind.

Obviously, when the time came for Adrian's visits, she would have to choose between the lesser of two evils—constant exposure to Adrian or rattling around in an empty house and missing the only family member she had. From his too-innocent expression, he'd already guessed which option she would favor.

"I'll admit we'll need a larger house," she began, "but it won't happen until I pay off my bills and save some money."

"I could help," he began.

She shook her head. "If Jeremy needs something beyond my means, I'll let you know. Until then, forget it."

She saw the unhappiness in his eyes and the disapproving set to his mouth, so she bargained. "I'll agree to keep the grill and the TV if I can reimburse you for my medication."

"Throw in the sofa, and you have a deal."

She hated being beholden to him, but it was so very nice and functional, even if it was a trifle too large. "OK, but no more purchases until we discuss them first."

"Agreed," he said. "Now that we've settled that, is there any chocolate cake left?"

"You're still hungry?"

"I'm a growing boy." He grinned as he bounded to his feet. "Would you like a piece?"

"I'll pass. I'm still stuffed from dinner."

As he disappeared in the kitchen to serve himself, she heard Jeremy stirring in the other room. Immediately she rose to check on him. When she saw he was restless and wouldn't go back to sleep on his own even with his pacifier, she cuddled him against her shoulder.

"Did you have a nightmare, my little man?" she crooned.

Adrian appeared beside her. "What's wrong?"

"Bad dream, I guess," she whispered. "In another minute he'll be asleep."

He was. She laid him in his crib and tiptoed out of the room after Adrian. Expecting him to say goodnight, she was surprised when he snaked both arms around her waist and captured her in his embrace.

"You know something?" he asked. "I always knew we'd make beautiful babies, and we did."

She smiled. "One, anyway."

"He is such a miracle."

"All babies are."

"I didn't have a chance to thank you for the past couple of days. They were...special."

"I'm glad someone had a good time," she said dryly, thinking of her miserable Sunday.

"I know you didn't, but I was able to experience what you go through on a twenty-four seven basis. I appreciate that you allowed me to take care of him instead of someone else. Whether you realize it or not, you gave me a gift beyond compare."

His sincerity touched her heart. "I'm glad," she said simply, before she grinned. "Hold that thought, though, when you're in the middle of a tie-score football game with your team on the five-yard line, and your son decides he's hungry or wants your undivided attention."

He chuckled. "Then I'll have to negotiate another deal with his mom."

"Really? Negotiate with what?"

"With this." He bent his head and kissed her.

She'd told herself how dangerous it would be to kiss him again and he'd proved her correct. In spite of the minefield still lying between them, his need ignited her own and she felt as if she were bursting into flame. Everything faded into the background, leaving her senses free to fully appreciate Adrian.

His warmth surrounded her as he tugged her close and pressed one hand against her spine so that she rested full length against him. He tasted of chocolate and smelled of sandalwood, and she felt a light rasp of five-o'clock shadow as he trailed kisses down her neck.

"I should go," he muttered against her skin.

"Probably," she agreed, although she didn't make any effort to break out of his hold. In fact, being in his arms was completely intoxicating. Sending him home seemed too horrible an act to contemplate.

"I don't want to." His hands roamed to the edge of her shirt. His fingers slipped under the fabric and skimmed the bare skin above the waistband of her Bermuda shorts.

"I don't want you to, either," she breathed, wondering if yesterday's migraine had caused her to lose her mind and all of her inhibitions. No, even if all her faculties were intact, she couldn't refuse him because she wanted their special brand of intimacy as much as he did.

Heaven help her.

His hands slowly inched upward until he reached the soft swells of her breasts. Instinctively, she arched her back to grant him fuller access, and a half-groan came from his throat.

"Do you know my real reasons for buying that sofa?" he asked.

"No."

"Because I imagined you sprawled on it. Wearing nothing but me."

"Hmmm."

"The colors reminded me of—"

"You're talking too much," she said breathlessly as his hands released the clasp of her bra.

"I am," he agreed.

"Make love to me, Adrian," she begged, noticing her voice sounded husky, as if it belonged to someone more exotic and alluring than everyday, average Sabrina.

"I thought you'd never ask."

Within minutes, their clothes disappeared and he lowered her onto the sofa cushions, fitting her body beneath his. His hands masterfully and magically made her body quiver. Needing to ground herself, she flung her arms around his neck and tried to ride out the building storm.

Suddenly, he pulled away. "Wait."

"For what?" She grumbled at the interruption.

He rustled through the clothing on the floor, dug in his jeans pocket and as soon as he removed a foil packet, she understood.

Fumbling with the package, he mumbled an un-complimentary "Damn" before she took pity on him and ripped it open herself. Although his clumsiness with protection didn't prove anything, his ten-thumbed dexterity seemed to corroborate his story that he hadn't seen anyone since she'd left. He was as out of practice as she was and the thought was comforting.

Yet, when he repositioned himself between her legs, ineptitude became skill, awkwardness became grace and every action became perfection, as if their instincts were so tuned to each other that months of celibacy didn't matter.

She squirmed beneath him, eager to receive him, begging him to hurry. When she thought she couldn't stand another second of this torment, he slipped inside her and she groaned with delight.

He moved slowly, then built to a steady rhythm that seemed choreographed specifically for them.

Suddenly she shattered as tsunami waves of pleasure surged through her. Another thrust sent Adrian surfing with her.

He collapsed, pressing her into the cushions, but she hardly noticed. It could have been a minute later, or an hour, but still buried deeply inside her, he raised himself on his elbows.

"I didn't mean to crush you."

"You didn't."

"I didn't hurt you, did I?"

He sounded so concerned she smiled. "I'm fine. More than fine, actually. I'm great."

He kissed her temple. "Me, too. That was amazing."

What she thought more amazing was how easily the barriers and hurts of the past year had disappeared during this magical interlude, although she didn't delude herself by thinking these moments signaled a happily-ever-after ending. Then an un-welcome thought popped into her head.

"Did you plan this?"

"No." He was aghast. "What makes you think I did?"

"The condom in your pocket."

His boyish smile appeared. "Wishful thinking on my part. Apparently my fairy godfather chose to grant my wish."

"I didn't know fairies were of the male persuasion."

"How else does one get little fairies?" he teased.

"How else, indeed?" she said wryly.

A car door slammed in the distance. "I suppose that's my cue to get up." He brushed a stray lock of hair off her cheek before he planted a swift, hard kiss on her mouth. "I must say, though, I feel like a teenager who's hoping his parents won't come home unexpectedly."

"The joys of necking in the living room."

"All the more reason to move," he countered. "As much as I enjoyed the sofa, I'd prefer a bed, especially in a room without impressionable ears."

"Aren't you assuming there will be a next time?" she asked as she dressed quickly, aware of Adrian doing the same.

"Yes, I am," he said boldly. "Which is why we need

to talk." He plopped back on the couch and patted the cushion beside him in an invitation to join him.

Suddenly wary, she sat at the opposite end. "About what?"

"About what comes next. I want to acknowledge Jeremy as my son."

She'd expected this discussion, but she'd hoped to postpone it for a few more weeks. While unveiling him as Jeremy's father wouldn't be easy and she didn't know what sort of reception he'd receive afterwards from the staff who'd taken her under their wings, she was willing to tell the world. "If you want to announce you're his father, go ahead, but I'd like some advance notice."

"I don't want to just go public," he said. "I want my position to be recognized legally."

She'd always anticipated his request and, in fact, she was surprised he'd warned her of his intention, but she'd hoped to postpone any official action for a while. Sharing Jeremy on paper seemed to bring her one step closer to losing control over her son's life. Apparently she suffered from the same control issues that Adrian did.

"Is it really necessary?" she asked. "I'm willing to work with you and I thought I'd proved it this past week."

"A verbal agreement isn't good enough. What if you met another guy and changed your mind? Moved to the other side of the country?"

She smiled at his concerns. Although she'd never admit it, no other man would ever compare to Adrian. "I won't."

He raised an eyebrow, as if unconvinced. "You also have Jeremy to consider. What if the unthinkable happened to you? What if you landed in the hospital, were in a car accident or became a victim, like our Jane Doe? Who would look after Jeremy? The bigger question is, who would know to contact me?"

As tempted as she was to play the odds that nothing untoward would ever happen, if the worst-case scenario did unfold, Jeremy would suffer the trauma of being left in limbo. She'd already considered that herself when their Jane Doe had walked through the ED doors.

"Do you have a will naming Jeremy's guardian?" he asked.

"No."

"Who's listed as next of kin on your medical and employment records?"

She'd been so determined to wipe all traces of Adrian out of her life that she'd left those spaces blank. An omission she'd already recognized but hadn't taken time to correct. "No one."

He paused. "You didn't list me as the father on his birth certificate either, did you?"

She'd completed the application form by printing "Unknown" in that particular blank. At the time she'd been intent on forgetting Adrian existed, although without him, Jeremy would never have been born.

"I refuse to feel guilty about my decision," she said stiffly. "You didn't want to be a part of my life, remember? Why would I mention you under those circumstances?"

He hesitated, as if carefully choosing his words. "The real question is, what do you want to do now?"

She had to give him credit for asking even though the determined lines on his face indicated he would take matters into his own hands if she didn't voluntarily acknowledge his rightful access to Jeremy.

"I'll make the changes you'd mentioned."

"And the legal issue? Modifying his birth certificate?"

Telling herself everything would work out, that she didn't have anything to fear, she nodded. "I'll take care of it."

"When?"

"Soon."

He frowned, eyes narrowed. "When?" he repeated, clearly impatient.

"Soon," she emphasized, already wondering how she would squeeze attorney's fees out of her too-tight budget. "Although, as I recall, you said we had several months before we had to address the legalities."

"The legal system grinds slowly; nothing happens overnight. The sooner we start the process the sooner Jeremy will be protected in a worst-case scenario."

Although he was right, it grated to hear him point out the obvious. "Fine. I will."

Adrian shifted positions to face her. "You know," he said, offhandedly, "there is another option."

"Another option?"

"We could get married."

Married! Her breath immediately caught in her throat. They were the words she'd heard in her dreams when Adrian swooped in to admit he'd always loved her and would take her away from all this à la Cinderella, but fairy-tales only existed in books and reality wasn't filled with emotional warm fuzzies. Her flash of excitement died as his sentence hung in the air like smog.

Sabrina felt his gaze as he waited for her reaction. Unfortunately, she didn't know if she was happy, sad, or just plain surprised, but the longer she thought about it, the more bitter-sweet his offer became.

She stared at him, trying to read his body language for a clue as to if he was simply trying to create a joke to lighten the mood or if he meant what he'd said. His steady and unflinching gaze indicated the latter and the prospect unnerved her. Surely she'd misread him. "Are you serious?"

"Very."

Sabrina couldn't think of an appropriate answer. "I don't know what to say."

"Say yes."

As if she could. "Is this a spur-of-the-moment suggestion, or—?"

"I've thought about this all day," he admitted. "Marriage would solve a lot of issues."

She wondered if he realized that suggesting marriage as a solution wasn't the way to win a girl's heart. Then again, he didn't want her heart. He wanted his son.

"Marriage would also create others," she pointed out. "You can still be the father Jeremy needs without having that particular piece of paper."

"We're going to have one piece of paper or another," he said firmly. "You can choose between a marriage certificate or a custody decree. The certificate would be a lot easier to obtain and we wouldn't have the third-party court system looking over our shoulders to ensure we obey the letter of the law as far as visitation schedules and child-support payments went."

He was a private man, so she understood why he hated the idea of dragging his personal affairs before judges and lawyers. "That's what prompted your idea? You're looking for an easy fix?"

He started to speak, then stopped, as if he'd realized how close he was to stepping into something nasty. "I want what's best for Jeremy," he said. "If there's a simple way to accomplish that, why not take advantage of it?"

"Because 'easy' isn't the same as 'best'."

"Jeremy needs us."

"And we'll be there for him," she said. "We don't have to live together to accomplish that objective."

"Do you really want to put Jeremy in a position where he has to explain why his parents aren't married?"

"We're talking about *our* relationship, Adrian. You say this is what Jeremy needs, but…but I can't marry someone who thinks of me as an obligation or a means to an end."

"I don't," he insisted.

She wasn't convinced. "Are you sure?"

"Hell, yes! Have you already forgotten what we've been doing on this sofa? That didn't feel like an obligation to me and from your moans, I'd say it didn't feel like that to you either."

He would have to remind her of her uninhibited response. "We had great times in bed before, too, but those weren't enough to hold us together, were they? What we had was just sex."

"Just...?" He ran his hand through his hair until a few strands had spiked. "You're accusing me of having casual sex?"

"No, but—"

"Or could it be you think I'm the sort who'd sleep with a woman in order to get what I want?"

She spoke without thinking. "I think you're willing to do whatever is necessary to achieve your goal." As soon as she heard herself, she realized she'd crossed the line.

As expected, his response was immediate. His nostrils flared, his eyes burned with anger, and his tone grew quiet—all warning signs of his temper erupting with hurricane-force fury. "Trust me, Sabrina, if I only wanted *my son*, I would have hauled you into court faster than you can blink. I certainly wouldn't have bothered to break in the sofa."

For a long, painful moment, she didn't answer. Even with Jeremy shaking his rattle and jabbering to himself, the silence between them was deafening. "Tell me this," she said quietly, "if Jeremy hadn't been born and everything else was equal, would you be asking me to marry you?" She raised an eyebrow.

The anger faded from his eyes and puzzlement replaced it. He started to speak, then stopped as if to weigh his words. "Probably not, but…"

Her head had warned her to expect this particular response but her heart had encouraged her to think positively. Now he'd confirmed what she'd believed—if not for Jeremy, they'd simply be two people who shared a past—and the ember of hope residing in her chest winked out, leaving a smoky trail of disappointment behind.

This wasn't the first time she'd been rejected in life, she consoled herself. Neither was it the first time Adrian had rejected her. If she hadn't wanted the truth, she should have kept her thoughts and her questions to herself.

Her gaze didn't waver as she nodded. "That's what I thought."

"Let me finish. No, marriage wasn't on my mind when I came here because all I could think about was finding an opportunity to talk to you. I didn't allow myself to plan after that because everything hinged on how you reacted and if you forgave me. Between the golf-ball incident and finding out about Jeremy, I moved into fast forward."

"Now you can return to normal speed," she said crisply. "It's commendable of you to sacrifice your future with a woman you love for Jeremy, but it's unnecessary. I don't want to marry you."

"We could make it work," he insisted.

"It's nice of you to want to try," she said politely, aware that he'd missed the perfect opportunity to tell her that *she* was the woman he loved. Because he didn't, she knew she'd made the right decision. "We're both saving ourselves a lot of grief."

"We'd be good together," he insisted. "We proved that tonight, right here on this very sofa."

But do you love me? She wanted to ask outright, but she'd learned her lesson—don't ask questions if you don't want the truth.

"We generate a lot of sparks," she agreed, "but what happens when the sparks burn out? A commitment should be based on more than parenthood because we certainly don't need to live together or share wedding rings for you to assume a father's role. Besides, we've only been talking to each other

for a week after a year's worth of hard feelings. We'd
be foolish to rush into a situation we'd later regret."

He leaned forward. "I care about you, Sabrina. I
really do. Maybe I did move faster than I should
have, but I won't rescind my proposal. Just think
about it. OK?"

Caring was nice, but she cared about Clay as well
as a host of other people from colleagues and staff
to patients. It didn't mean she should marry them.

"We'll see," she said, aware she hadn't technically agreed to weigh his offer. She had to hear
three magical words before she'd alter her decision.
Only time would tell if he'd say them.

CHAPTER EIGHT

AFTER the conversation that hadn't gone as well as Adrian had hoped, he hated to leave. Once the door closed behind him, she wouldn't waste a minute of her time considering the possibilities. Knowing how devoted she was to Jeremy, he'd hoped the what's-best-for-Jeremy argument would carry more weight than if he'd professed how much he wanted her for himself. His strategy clearly hadn't netted the instant results he'd wanted.

Although he hadn't planned to make love with Sabrina before asking her to marry him, the timing had seemed perfect. Obviously she'd decided that he'd only been scratching an itch.

He didn't blame her for being wary. It *was* far-fetched to believe a man who'd disappeared from her life a year ago would have suddenly and miraculously had an epiphany after being reunited for a week. Perhaps when she calmed down and re-flected on their conversation—that he didn't *have* to sleep with her to gain access to his son—she'd take his proposal more seriously.

He hadn't realized it before, but he'd plainly poked the bruises of her self-esteem issues and had to wait for the pain to fade. Meanwhile, he'd insert himself into every aspect of her life and slowly chip away at her defenses.

As luck would have it, Jeremy helped matters along when he woke up inconsolable a few minutes later. Adrian couldn't leave.

Sabrina touched his forehead. "He feels warm. I wonder if he's teething again." The baby tugged at his ear and bellowed.

"Or he has an earache," Adrian offered.

Jeremy immediately held out his chubby little arms to Adrian and leaned out of Sabrina's hold with large tears clinging to his eyelashes.

"You'd better take him," Sabrina said. "It's obvious he wants you."

As soon as she'd handed him the baby, Adrian sat in the recliner and waited for Sabrina to return with a cold gel-filled plastic ring designed to soothe sore little gums. Jeremy greedily gnawed on it like a dog with its favorite bone.

"I hope you have more where this one came from," he said lightly.

"In the freezer. Would you like me to take him now?"

"I don't mind holding him. He's starting to settle down so the less jostling the better, don't you think?"

"Yes, but it's getting late and you—"

"I'm fine right here," he said.

"But you have to go to work in the morning."

"So do you."

"I can handle him by myself."

For some reason, Sabrina seemed determined to prove herself and he was tired of her believing he was always looking to find fault with her parenting skills. Would they never get past that?

"I know you can, but why should you when we can share the load?" he asked calmly. "This way we both get some sleep."

She hesitated and he tried harder. "How about this? I'll stick around to take the first shift and you can take the second."

"OK," she finally said. "Wake me when it's my turn."

In the end, he didn't have to. By one a.m., Jeremy's pain had subsided enough for him to sleep, and although there was plenty of time for

Adrian to drive to his apartment and catch a few winks in a comfortable bed, he didn't. With his clothes still in the car from his excursion to the dry cleaner's earlier in the day, his toothbrush and electric razor still in Sabrina's bathroom from the weekend, he had everything he possibly needed within reach.

Other than a bed, of course. Not wanting to risk upsetting Sabrina if she found him lying next to her, he grabbed an extra pillow and stretched out on the sofa.

Amazingly enough, Sabrina didn't seem surprised to find him there the next morning when she walked through on her way to the kitchen for Jeremy's bottle. She'd simply said, "The bathroom is free for the next fifteen minutes."

Even more amazing was how the next evening was a repeat of the one before.

"Why is it that his teeth only bother him at night?" Sabrina muttered at eleven o'clock as she paced the floor with Jeremy in her arms.

"It could be worse," Adrian said as he took a few minutes to flip through the twenty-four-hour television news channels to catch up on any world or national events he'd missed.

"How?"

"He could be fussy from the time we get home, but he waits until after we've had a nice, relaxing evening, a walk around the block or through the park, and a fun-filled swim in the sink."

Call him a masochist, but he was quite happy with Jeremy's schedule and if he didn't know better, he'd think the baby had planned it this way. Adrian was now spending the night without resistance, his clothes hung in Sabrina's closet rather than in his car, his underwear and socks were tucked in the bottom dresser drawer, and his shoes shared floor space with her tennis shoes, sandals, and high heels.

The only thing that would make him happier would be if the ring he'd purchased today was displayed on her finger rather than buried inside the outer pocket of his suitcase which he'd stored under her bed.

Actually, there was another thing that would make him happy, too—if he didn't sleep alone.

Even so, he wasn't complaining. With luck, Sabrina would realize just how handy he was to have around and his worries would be over.

He clicked off the TV with the remote control. "Do you want me to take him for a while?"

"Thanks, but it's my turn for the first shift," she

said. "You can sack out on my bed because you won't get any sleep if you stay out here."

"Are you sure?"

"Yeah. I didn't change the sheets, though, so if you want fresh linen, you can strip the bed yourself."

She shouldn't have used the word "strip" because it evoked all sorts of pleasant images. Knowing he'd also be surrounded by her scent as he lay on her pillows, he doubted if he'd sleep at all. If he did, he'd have the most erotic dreams of his entire life. "It's fine the way it is," he said instead. "Goodnight."

"Goodnight. Oh, I forgot to ask. Did you ever get in touch with Clay?"

"I left a voice message. I'm sure he'll call me tomorrow."

They had an unwritten rule of touching base with each other every few days, especially after Clay had moved into his own apartment. Clay had balked at first, but after Adrian had appeared unexpectedly on his doorstep during a most inopportune time when Clay was "entertaining" a pretty young woman, he'd agreed.

"OK. Goodnight."

He sank onto her bed and, as he'd imagined, his keen sense of smell detected Sabrina's trademark gingery citrus scent in the room. This could have been his for the last year if he hadn't screwed things up—if he hadn't felt so guilty over Clay's accident and been so determined to pay for his sins alone. In the end, Sabrina had paid for them, too.

Confessing his innermost thoughts had never been easy for him and it had only gotten worse after his parents had died. Although his aunts, teachers and other well-meaning neighbors had encouraged him to open up, he couldn't. Describing his father's last moments, talking about the promise he'd made, and voicing his fears, only cultivated his sense of being powerless and out of control. So, as the proverbial man of the house, he'd continued to hide his emotions behind silence and stoicism, noticing how his training had come in handy for those times when he had to deliver bad news to patients or their family members.

Unfortunately, his reticence wasn't helping mend his relationship with Sabrina and he wanted to mend it badly. With a son to consider, he wanted to rekindle the tender feelings they'd had for each other.

Unfortunately, it would take time for Sabrina to believe he had special care for her. Trust wasn't earned overnight, although he wished otherwise.

* * *

By Friday, Sabrina had to face facts. Adrian had moved in, lock, stock, and barrel. His change of residence was unofficial, of course, because he hadn't asked and she hadn't given permission. It had simply happened, taking place over the several days since her migraine attack. A single scrub suit in her closet suddenly became two weeks' worth of scrub suits and casual dress apparel. Both white and dark socks were tucked in the same drawer as Jeremy's undershirts and one-piece body suits. Adrian had even started to hang his toothbrush next to hers on the special holder instead of using his travel case.

He was there for the duration.

She should ask him to leave. It was too distracting to "play house" with him when she knew his reason for moving in. It was simple, really. He intended to prove they could make their marriage work by giving her a taste of the future as he saw it. No doubt he'd thought a woman who'd been raised by relatives who hadn't wanted her would jump at the chance to have her own family.

Sadly, he was right.

But she wasn't going to sacrifice her self-esteem to have that family. She wouldn't marry him, no matter how enticing the prospect was and no matter how hard he tried to convince her otherwise. Until he left, she simply had to protect herself emotionally and hope that when that day came, she'd handle it with grace and aplomb.

Meanwhile, she couldn't deny the gift of time that he provided. She could indulge in a leisurely bubble bath, read the newspaper or paint her toenails without waiting until Jeremy was asleep. She could sweep the floor without Jeremy perched on one hip. She could also retrieve her mail from the box at the curb without dashing down the sidewalk and keeping one ear open in case her son should notice her missing. She could actually run to the store by herself and not juggle a baby with her purchases.

Best of all, Adrian shared night-time duty so she was assured of a few hours of sleep each night.

Selfishly, she decided to let things ride while warning herself to remain objective and not grow attached to these temporary living arrangements.

But after watching the joy appear on Adrian's face as he put Jeremy to bed or helped bundle him off to day care, she didn't have the heart to take those simple pleasures away from him. That loss would come soon enough when he returned to Denver.

Fortunately, his departure was a problem for

another day. The one facing her now was far more immediate.

"Someone made a mistake with my paycheck," Sabrina told the hospital's Accounts Receivable clerk. "The net amount doesn't reflect my payroll deduction for my hospital bill."

As soon as Sabrina had opened her direct deposit pay stub envelope, she'd been surprised to note the net amount was far greater than it had been since her last check two weeks ago. Knowing she wasn't due a raise for some time, she examined the deductions until she found a crucial one missing.

The girl clicked a few computer keys, then shook her head. "According to this, your account is paid in full."

"That's impossible," she said flatly. "I still have two years to go."

"My computer says otherwise."

"There has to be a mistake. Someone else's payment must have been posted because I didn't—"

"There's no mistake. A check was received and the money credited to your account."

Adrian, she thought irritably. How could he do this when she'd made it plain she didn't need his help? OK, maybe she could use a temporary boost in her finances, but she didn't *want* it coming from him. Somehow it made her feel beholden when she craved her independence.

"If you'll give me a second, I can give you more information." The clerk studied her screen. "Here it is. According to this, the balance was paid last week. Friday, to be exact."

She thought back to their conversation on Monday and how money had been discussed, but only in the most general terms. And even if she'd been specific, Adrian couldn't be responsible if her bill had been paid on the previous Friday. For all he'd known, her health insurance had covered all her expenses.

"Can you tell who paid it?"

"Sorry. All I have is a copy of a cashier's check made out to the hospital with your name in the memo line."

Sabrina could hardly take in her good fortune. Things like this didn't normally happen to her. "I wish I knew who it was. I'd love to thank them."

"Check with Alice. She's the one who handles the actual posting. Maybe she'll remember details."

"Thanks. I will."

Alice, however, wasn't helpful either. "An attorney brought it by. Said one of his clients had wanted to give an anonymous donation to you, so I didn't question him."

"Isn't it against hospital policy for staff to receive gifts from patients?"

"Yes, but technically I can't prove the gift came from a patient, so if I were you, I'd take the money and run." She grinned. 'Honestly, the bean counters aren't concerned about *who* pays the bill, only that it gets paid. And yours is."

"Who was the attorney?"

Alice was apologetic. "Sorry. He didn't mention his name and as I don't run in legal circles, I didn't recognize him. If I were you, though, I'd say a prayer for the person responsible."

"Oh, I will," she assured Alice. "Don't worry."

As she walked from the accounting department, her mind raced with possibilities of what she could do with the extra money each month. She could finally have a mechanic diagnose the strange knock in her car's engine, replace her lumpy recliner, or just save her money for a larger apartment. Better yet, she could apply it to her other loan and pay it off sooner.

By the time she returned to the ED, she still hadn't come down from her financial windfall high.

"Good news?" Adrian asked as she approached the nurses' station.

"The best," she said with a smile. "Excellent, in fact. So excellent that we're going to celebrate. Any requests for the weekend?"

"Celebrate? Wow. What happened? You didn't win the lottery, did you?"

She giggled. "Almost, but not quite. Someone paid off my hospital bill and it wasn't a small amount either."

"No kidding. Who would do such a thing?"

"I don't know. It was an anonymous donation, but…" she smiled "…I'll take it and rejoice in my unknown benefactor's generosity. So, what do you say we find a sitter and go someplace nice for dinner?"

"I'm game. Where do you have in mind?"

"How does Mexican food sound? I'm hungry for a beef enchilada smothered in cheese," she confessed.

"Perfect." He glanced at the wall clock. "Things are quiet for the moment, so I'm headed to Radiology."

"Still waiting for the MRI results on the patient in room three?" At his nod, she continued, "Do you really think the scans will show something they didn't a week ago?" Alan Cavendish had been brought in by his wife for the second time in as many weeks because of severe headaches and dizzy spells. Sabrina had arranged for a second scan before she'd slipped away to straighten out her paycheck problems.

"Who knows? He came in at the end of my shift last week and the evening-shift doc handled his case. According to the records, he was treated for migraine and released. So, if he's still having a problem, something's going on. I intend to convince the radiologist to move my case to the top of his to-be-read pile and to go over it with a fine-toothed comb."

"I can do that for you," she offered.

"Thanks, but I'd like to see the fellow myself." He grinned. "The coffee over there is better than ours anyway and I'm hoping to bum a cup off them." He strolled away, whistling.

A few minutes later, just as she was about to check on Mr Cavendish, the exam-room door opened and his wife nearly knocked her over in her rush.

"Thank God you're here," she said, her eyes wide. "He's having a seizure."

Sabrina pushed past her and in a brief glance saw her husband's clenched jaw and twitching movements. "Pull the call cord," she instructed the woman as she began first aid until Adrian or one of the physicians' assistants arrived.

Cavendish was already in a bed with the rails raised, so she didn't have to worry about him falling, but vomiting could be a problem, so she rolled him onto his side to prevent the possibility of aspiration.

During her initial assessment, both he and his wife had denied this question, but she had to ask again. "He hasn't had any seizures before, has he?"

"No. None. Is he going to be OK?"

"We'll do everything we can." Sabrina held him in place as best she could, trying to keep his arms from banging on the aluminum side rails while she noted his respirations.

The door opened and Hilary came in, took one look, and said, "I'll get Doctor," before she scurried out and returned a minute later with Adrian.

"How long?" he asked tersely.

"Since you went to Radiology."

Grimly, he glanced at Hilary as he inclined his head in Mrs Cavendish's direction. "He'll need help, then." He rattled off a dosage while Hilary gently guided Alan's shocked wife from the room.

Sabrina hated to question his order but she wanted to be sure she hadn't misunderstood. "That's a high dose," she commented.

His gaze steadily met hers. "I know."

"OK." Sabrina pulled the medication from the

drug cart, double-checked the vial's label before she drew off the required amount, then injected it into Cavendish's IV port.

At first nothing happened, then gradually Cavendish's seizure eased under their watchful eyes. Sabrina gently rolled him onto his back and covered him with a blanket.

"Did you get your report?"

He nodded, his expression still grim.

Headaches, dizziness, and now a seizure added up to a serious problem. "What did the test show?"

"Brain tumor."

Her heart sank. "Oh, no. How bad is it?"

"All brain tumors are bad."

"I know, but is it operable?"

"Mr Cavendish will need a lot more tests before the neurosurgeon can decide." He heaved a sigh. "In the meantime, call whichever neurologist, neurosurgeon and oncologist is available and arrange for a transfer to a medical floor."

"Will do."

"Oh, and schedule him for the next available EEG while I break the news to his wife."

The electroencephalogram would record the electrical activity in the brain and convert those impulses into a tracing pattern which would then reflect the state of the brain. A tumor or other structural abnormality would shortcircuit those impulses, giving valuable information as to the location of the growth. She hoped Cavendish's tumor would be treatable.

Sabrina contacted the on-call neuro people and spent the rest of the afternoon in a flurry of doctors' orders and test procedures while monitoring her patient and giving moral support to Alan's wife. By the end of the afternoon, his doctors were trying to decide between surgery and radiation or a combination of the two.

Although this wasn't the first tragic case Sabrina had ever encountered, this one affected her more than most. Young people, young couples, always tugged at her heart.

She quietly went about her business and when she got home she gave Jeremy an extra-long cuddle until he eventually squealed a protest.

"My turn," Adrian said with a smile as he took Jeremy from her.

"Maybe we shouldn't go out tonight," she said.

"Why not? We're celebrating, remember?"

"I know, but I just feel as if we…shouldn't. It just seems so *wrong* to have a good time when people like the Cavendishes are in crisis mode."

"Moping won't change their situation," he told her.

"I suppose not." She let out a long breath. "OK, we'll go."

Yet as they sat in the fragrantly spicy atmosphere of Casa Ramon, enjoying a Mariachi band and eating their way through an appetizer of chips and three kinds of salsa as well as their dinner entrees, she realized Adrian's mood was more quiet and somber than usual and she wondered why.

Was he more upset over the Cavendish case than he'd admitted? In all the time she'd known him, he'd never acted as if the tragedies he'd encountered at the hospital had ever weighed him down, although she did remember a few times when he'd been quiet and withdrawn. Naturally, he'd given any number of excuses for his mood—he was tired, had nothing to say, etc. and she'd accepted them without question.

However, now she wondered if he'd felt the same sadness and disappointment as everyone else. Could it be that he'd simply been suffering in silence and hadn't wanted her, or anyone else for that matter, to know just how deeply he felt about his patients? That sort of behavior would certainly have ruined his tough, nothing-bothers-me macho image. The more she pondered, the more she could examine his character in a completely different light.

"Do you want to talk about it?" she asked softly.

He looked startled. "Talk about what?"

"Whatever's bothering you."

"Nothing's bothering me."

She'd heard that one before. "You're quiet."

"It's been a long day."

That, too, was a familiar refrain.

She spoke as if he'd answered her question. Instead of receiving encouragement, she chose to give it. "Alan Cavendish is in good hands. Dr Graham is an excellent oncologist and all the staff think highly of Dr James's neurosurgery skills."

"So I've heard."

"Did you know Alan and Nicole—that's his wife—have a two-year-old daughter? Apparently they'd been married for years and weren't able to have children, and then, bingo, along comes Lily."

"Did Jeremy do anything special today at day care?"

His abrupt change of subject suggested that she'd hit a sore spot. "He's seven months old, Adrian. He eats, sleeps and plays with his toys."

"He's due for a lot of 'firsts', Bree," he said, as if she needed a reminder.

"True, but—"

"He could crawl any day," he said, sounding determined to focus the conversation on someone other than himself. "You can tell from looking at him that he's eager to go, but he hasn't quite figured out how to start his engine yet."

Sweet baby Jane! How self-absorbed had she been to not have recognized his distraction techniques for what they were? How many other patients had caused him to internalize his struggles because he wouldn't talk about them? In fact, she now suspected why he'd been so close-lipped about Clay's accident, especially when he'd helped pay for the motorcycle in the first place. It had been too painful and the drastic events had only reinforced Adrian's lack of control over the situation.

She leaned across the table to place her hand on his forearm, noting his tense muscles. "It's OK to be upset about our patient. You don't have to hide it from me."

"I'm not upset." He fingered the condensation on his bottle. "We've seen thousands of cases like his. Life is short and doesn't come with any guarantees. Period."

"Life *is* short, especially for some," she agreed, "but that doesn't mean we shouldn't feel badly at the injustice."

He studied a point over her shoulder for several

drawn-out seconds before he met her gaze. The pain in his eyes caused her heart to ache. But before she could think of something to say, he wiped all expression off his face.

"Can we go?" he asked abruptly.

"Sure. Just let me ask the waiter for the—"

"I got it." He rose, pulled out his wallet and tossed enough bills on the table to cover the meal and a generous tip.

"This was my treat, remember?" she said as he ushered her to his vehicle as quickly as if they were racing to attend a code blue.

"Considering all the meals I've eaten at your house, I owe you." He opened her car door.

"You don't owe me anything," she said, sliding inside. "We had a nice dinner by ourselves and in wonderful surroundings."

"When do we have to relieve Kate?"

Kate was babysitting and she'd pulled Sabrina aside before they'd left the house to whisper her willingness to stay as late as Sabrina needed her…then she'd winked.

"Whenever," she said airily. "I have a television now so Kate won't be bored after Jeremy goes to sleep."

"There's a walking trail around my apartment

complex," he said. "Do you mind if we go there for a while?"

He obviously needed physical activity to release his tension. She was glad he'd suggested walking rather than working out at the gym because she'd rather be outdoors. "Not at all."

Within twenty minutes they were moving along the paved walkway at a steady clip. Thank goodness her sandals were comfortable enough for walking, although if she'd suspected he'd planned a workout this evening, she would have worn her exercise clothes instead of a denim skirt and sleeveless blouse.

"It's a lovely evening," she said as they passed through a shady grove of oak trees. "Not many people out yet, I see."

She tried to keep up with his long-legged stride, but after she began huffing and puffing and earned a stitch in her side, she gave up and came to a dead stop. "That's it. If you want to play the tortoise and the hare, I'm game. When you're finished loping around the path, you can come back to me."

"Sorry."

As soon as she caught her breath, she started off and this time he matched her pace rather than set it.

Once again she waited for him to initiate conversation and when he didn't, she took matters into her own hands and played on a hunch.

"Tell me about your parents," she said.

"They're both dead. You know that."

She nodded. "I also know you raised your brother and sisters, but what were your folks like? Did they laugh a lot, get along with each other? Did your dad take you fishing, teach you how to change the oil in your car, or scold you if you stayed out too late?"

He thought for a minute. "I remember Mom being happy all the time. She gave lots of hugs and baked the best peanut-butter cookies. She let me flatten them right out of the oven with a fork. If I had to describe her, I'd say she was more of a free spirit, artsy type."

"She sounds wonderful."

"Dad, on the other hand, was serious, although Mom always could get him to smile. He wasn't a talkative guy, but his love for us showed in the things he did and taught us. He always made time when we needed him. He was a good man, a hard worker, our biggest fan at baseball and football games, and he drilled responsibility into us. After his accident, I stepped into his shoes."

"It sounds as if he had big shoes to fill."

"To an eighteen year-old, they were *huge*. They still are, in fact."

"Did Clay and your sisters balk at you being in charge?"

"Not really. The girls had the usual teenage histrionics and angst, but my aunts helped me handle those episodes. Everything worked out in the end. We all earned college degrees, have good jobs, and didn't land in jail." He grinned. "Not bad, if I say so myself."

"I'd have to agree." She threaded her arm through his as they strolled down the path. If their relaxed pace reflected his mood, then their near-Olympic sprint had been the perfect means to release some of his frustration.

The cicadas sang louder and for several minutes Sabrina simply listened to the sounds of nature and enjoyed the sense of companionship she felt as she remained tucked against his side.

The pastoral setting convinced her to bring up the subject he wanted to avoid. "What do you think of Alan Cavendish's chances?"

Adrian tensed ever so slightly and if she hadn't been hanging onto his arm like a leech, she never would have known. "Not good."

"How do you feel about that?"

"You're a psychologist now?"

"Just someone who's concerned about you."

"Don't be. There's nothing either of us can say that will make a difference."

From Adrian's flat tone, Alan Cavendish's diagnosis had clearly hit Adrian hard, either for the same reasons as hers or because his earlier test results hadn't indicated such a serious problem. Whatever the cause, she wanted to comfort a man who needed comforting but didn't want it.

Sensing he wouldn't appreciate the usual platitudes, she simply held onto him and refused to let go. The cicadas' song faded into the background as she stroked Adrian's arm in an effort to soothe him when words seemed trite.

"No, but it might make a difference to *you*. You must have a thought or an impression of some sort."

He stopped. "My thoughts and impressions are my own."

Once again he was shutting her out and she was slowly seeing a pattern. "Venting is better than bottling up your frustration. I, for one, am very frustrated and angry about the situation."

He didn't answer, so she pressed on. "But, then, I have to ask myself, if we'd diagnosed him a week sooner, would it have made a difference? Would it?" she demanded.

"Maybe. Maybe not," he admitted.

"No matter what, you did your best."

"Did I?" He turned a wounded gaze on her. "I turned him over to someone else so I could go home."

"The evening physician is every bit as capable as you. He's the one who interpreted the results."

"Last week's report stated 'No abnormalities found'," Adrian said. "This week the radiologist found the spot so he compared the two sets of scans. The lesion had been there all along."

"Oh, dear."

"No kidding."

"Hindsight is always twenty-twenty," she told him.

"The point is, whether a week would have made a difference or not, we shouldn't have made the mistake."

"Maybe the radiologist was tired when he read the first set of pictures. Maybe he had a stack of films waiting and was in a hurry. Maybe he was interrupted and thought he'd come back to it and for some reason never did. Maybe the transcriptionist confused her cases. Who knows? There could be any number of extenuating circumstances. You weren't to blame."

"I still feel somewhat responsible."

"You can't take on the entire world, Adrian, even if you think you should. Did—?"

"Can we talk about something else?" he asked impatiently. "A topic other than medicine?"

Oh…damn it! She'd finally made progress but he'd clammed up before her eyes. Still, Rome wasn't built in a day… "If that's what you want."

They'd come full circle and stopped in front of his building. As he hesitated, she asked, "Do you want another jaunt around the complex or should we go home?"

"Come inside with me."

He stood tall and stoic, waiting for her reply with a plea in his eyes. Immediately and without hearing specifics, she knew what he wanted. He could deny it with his last breath, but he was hurting and needed her to help him feel less subject to the whims of fate and more in control.

She rose on tiptoe to brush a soft kiss against his mouth. "Last one in is a rotten egg."

CHAPTER NINE

ADRIAN'S apartment hadn't changed since she'd been here last, although now his belongings were noticeably absent. It still resembled a hotel and had that same, unaired, vacant quality, but at the moment she didn't care because it had one major point in its favor.

Privacy.

The minute the door closed behind her, he took her in his arms and kissed her with a starving-man greediness that caught her by surprise and raised her spirits. He wanted *her*.

She tugged on his shirt as he did likewise, but before she could do more than unsnap his shorts, he'd hoisted her into the air. She gasped from the sudden weightlessness, only to realize he was carrying her into the bedroom.

"We're going to do this right," he mumbled against her mouth.

"The sofa would have…" she gasped as he nipped her neck "…been fine," she finished when she caught her breath.

"Not this time."

Somehow, without ever breaking contact, clothes disappeared and the comforter sailed onto the floor a few seconds before he followed her onto the slick, cool sheets and covered her body with his.

He made love with a desperation she recognized and understood, giving of herself freely until he found his release. When it was over, when he'd collapsed on the sheets beside her, she simply snuggled against him.

He flung one arm over his eyes. "I'm sorry."

"What for?" she asked, although she knew.

"I went too fast."

"Am I complaining?"

"No."

"Then don't worry about it." She craned her neck to see his expression. "There's always next time."

"True." He squeezed her arm.

Deciding she could get away with asking a few questions now that he was relaxed and his defenses were down, she did. "Your dad didn't encourage you to show your emotions, did he?"

"He wasn't a demonstrative sort, more of an introspective, quiet type. I've been told I take after him," he said wryly.

"Oh, I don't know." She traced a circle on his chest. "You can be demonstrative and noisy on occasion. Like now. Or when you're with Jeremy."

"That's different."

"Is it?"

"Of course it is. What patient wants to see their doctor blubbering all over him? People lose faith if I can't be objective."

"True, but that doesn't mean you can't share your worries and concerns with someone. It isn't healthy to bottle all your feelings up inside. People aren't supposed to suffer alone."

"Speaking of suffering…" he flipped her on top of him "…I have this ache."

She felt his body's response and smiled. "How bad is it?"

"Bad enough we'll have to take it slow and easy."

She threaded her arms behind his neck. "If you say so. I always follow doctor's orders."

"I'm worried about you," Kate told Sabrina on Sunday after she and Adrian had returned home from finishing their round of golf. Adrian had gone to the back yard so he could call Clay and enjoy an uninterrupted conversation.

"What do you mean?"

"Aren't you two getting rather chummy? He's only been in town for two weeks."

Sabrina smiled, touched by her friend's concern. "I know, but—"

"And, honestly, I wasn't snooping, but when I put Jeremy down for his nap, well…" she grimaced "…it's obvious he's moved in with you."

"He has."

"Oh, Sabrina." Kate's distress shone as brightly as a neon sign. "Aren't you rushing things? I mean, you're a single mom with a baby who hasn't celebrated his first birthday. Do you want to run the risk of having a second?"

While Sabrina would dearly love Jeremy to have a sibling, she wasn't foolish enough to provide him with one within weeks of Adrian resurfacing in her life. "You worry too much."

"Of course I do. That's what friends are for. Whatever you do," she begged, "don't forget the last guy you dated. He left you high and dry and—"

"He's outside."

Kate stopped short and blinked owlishly. "Who's outside?"

"The guy who left me high and dry."

She frowned. "Adrian's outside."

Sabrina smiled. "Exactly."

Understanding crept across Kate's features. "Oh. My. God. Are you telling me—?"

"Yes."

"The creep who ran out on you is the hospital's current heartthrob stud muffin?"

Sabrina nodded. "That's him."

Kate sank bonelessly onto the sofa. "Oh. My. God," she repeated. "You actually let him back into your life?"

"I didn't have a choice. He *is* Jeremy's father."

Kate stared at her, clearly stupefied. "I can't believe this."

"It is rather unbelievable."

"If we hadn't been through so much together, I wouldn't ask, but what happened?" Kate's eyes grew saucer-sized. "Please don't tell me you had a one-night stand."

Sabrina perched on the edge of the recliner. "We were dating, rather seriously I thought, but our relationship fell apart after his brother landed in hospital." She told the entire story, beginning with Adrian's fatefully misguided decision to her arrival in Pinehaven.

By the end, Kate was plainly stunned. "Oh, Sabrina. What are you going to do next?"

Jeremy threw his ring of plastic keys on the floor and while Sabrina retrieved them, she pondered her answer.

"I'm not sure." She hesitated. "He's asked me to marry him."

Kate's gaze grew intent. "Is that what you want?"

Sabrina shrugged as she balanced Jeremy on her lap and breathed in his baby scent.

"Do you love him?"

She didn't waver. "Yes. I almost wish I didn't, but I do."

"And that means…?" Kate raised an eyebrow.

"It means nothing," she said firmly. "My feelings are one-sided. Adrian doesn't love me."

Kate frowned. "Are you sure?"

Sabrina rolled her eyes. "Does the sun set in the west? Of course I'm positive."

"So what are you going to do? It isn't wise to let him stay here."

"From my perspective, it isn't," she agreed. "But he's good for Jeremy, so what else *can* I do? I'll just have to tolerate the situation for my son's sake."

Kate rose. "I don't know, dearie. If you ask me,

you're setting yourself up for a major meltdown, but whatever happens, I'm here for you."

"Thanks, Kate. You're the best friend ever."

The back door squeaked, followed by the squish of Adrian's tennis shoes on the linoleum floor. "Let me know if you have any problems with the situation we just discussed," Kate said as Adrian appeared in the living room. "One of my former patients comes from a family with mob connections. She had a difficult delivery and the grateful parents will be more than happy to do a favor for me." She glanced pointedly at Adrian.

Sabrina smiled. "I'll keep it in mind."

Kate leaned over and kissed Jeremy's head. "See you later, short stuff. Any time you need a sitter, let me know. And, Adrian…" her smile was too sweet. "Do you have a bulletproof vest?"

His brow furrowed. "No, why?"

"Just wondering," she said airily. "Take care and I'll see you later."

"Mob connections and bulletproof vests?" Adrian asked with stunned curiosity as Kate walked toward her car. "What was that about?"

"I think she was delivering a warning."

"Why? What did I do?"

"You moved in," she said wryly.

"Ahh."

"I also told her you were Jeremy's father."

He nodded slowly. "Makes sense. She can finally put a name and a face to the 'dirty rotten scoundrel who left you high and dry when you were pregnant'," he said dryly.

"I hate to agree, but yes."

"I assume every move I make will be scrutinized from now on?"

"Probably. Does it bother you?"

He shrugged. "I have nothing to hide."

"Things might be a little chilly for you at work," she said. "You should prepare yourself."

"I can handle it."

She didn't doubt it at all. Adrian had charmed the staff since he'd arrived, so a few might study him with curiosity and wariness, but he'd win them over again.

"Did you get in touch with Clay?" she asked.

"Yeah. He finally answered his phone." He held out his arms to Jeremy and the little scamp giggled and dove forward for Adrian to catch him.

"How's he been?"

Adrian sat on the sofa and laid Jeremy on his lap in order to tickle his tummy. "He claims he's fine. Said his stomach has been acting up the past few days. He thinks he contracted some sort of food poisoning from a little taco stand he visited."

"Did he see a doctor?"

He shook his head. "According to him, he's doing better."

"Do you want to drive to Denver and check on him?" she asked. "It's early enough. We can."

He looked thoughtful for moment. "I'd like to, but I know he'll get upset if I do." He grinned. "Who wants to have his big brother running over to check on him just because he has a stomachache and diarrhea?"

She laughed as she sat beside her men. "Not the best time to have a visitor."

"Exactly. I'll call him tomorrow. Maybe we could plan to drive to Denver next weekend. We both have four days off."

She leaned over. "Hear that, Jeremy? You're going to have your first road trip."

"We could make it a honeymoon." He sounded hopeful.

"Why should we?" She didn't just want a *good* reason, she wanted the *right* reason.

"I'm introducing Jeremy to my family. It would be nice to introduce my wife at the same time."

Wrong answer. "Ah, the kill-two-birds-with-one-stone philosophy. Well, it would be nice if I won the lottery, too, but that isn't going to happen."

"You're being stubborn." He spoke without rancor, almost as if he hadn't expected her to agree, but had felt obliged to ask…just in case.

"I'm being prudent."

"For how long?"

"I try my best to always be prudent," she said primly, aware she hadn't answered his question.

"I can't believe you won't do what's best for Jeremy." He spoke calmly, without any trace of surprise or anger, which indicated he was fishing.

"Save your guilt trip," she advised. "Besides, I don't understand your rush. You're enjoying the perks of married life. You have a son, a pseudo-wife—and don't think I haven't noticed how you've given up sleeping on the sofa every night."

Ever since they'd warmed the sheets in his apartment on Friday, he'd taken it on himself to slide into bed beside her at the end of each day. She wasn't complaining, but that evening had effectively ended an on-again, off-again sleeping arrangement.

"Plus," she continued, "you're still able to leave any time you'd like."

"What if I don't intend to go?"

She hesitated, hating to raise her hopes. "Is that

your plan? To give up everything you have in Denver, including your family, to move here, where I have a job I love and friends who support me?"

At his hesitation, she smiled weakly. "I didn't think so."

"I can draw up whatever custody arrangements you'd like, Ms. Hollister." Jonathan Gray steepled his fingers as he peered at her over his reading glasses. "The problem comes in asking the other party to sign them."

"This is a fair arrangement, isn't it? Jeremy's father can visit any time he wishes, but I keep sole custody."

"Have you discussed these terms with Dr McReynolds? Is he agreeable to them?"

She thought of the conversation that had led to her scheduling an appointment with a lawyer. "We haven't talked specifics," she admitted.

"I suggest you do, Ms. Hollister. While your offer seems generous, the family court in our county rarely awards sole custody until a parent is proven as unfit. Can you do that?"

Adrian, an unfit parent? Hardly. He could be the featured parent on fatherhood posters. "No. Definitely not."

"Then the court will most likely award joint custody. It can be joint legal custody in which you and Dr McReynolds share in any decisions regarding your son, or joint physical custody, in which case you share in the physical care and lodging with each of you having equal time."

"So Jeremy would have two homes."

"Basically. Although as young as he is, you might be granted primary physical custody. Keep in mind, though, if it's granted, Jeremy's father can ask the court to reconsider when Jeremy gets older. My advice is for the two of you to sit down and devise a parenting plan that specifies your agreed-on arrangement. Without it, the court will decide what they feel is in Jeremy's best interests. You may or may not like their ruling."

So much for this being a simple matter. "I see," she said.

"Tell me, has Dr McReynolds supported you in any way, either during your pregnancy or after?"

"No." She thought a moment, then backpedaled. "Though lately he's bought a few things for Jeremy and for our house."

"Hmmm. We could make the argument that he hasn't supported you and therefore you'd like primary physical custody, but the court takes a dim

view of fathers who don't live up to their responsibilities."

Dad drilled responsibility into us.

Adrian's comment reverberated in her head. If
not for his sense of responsibility, she wouldn't be
sitting in an attorney's office now, looking at ways
to change the status quo. That same sense of duty
would interfere with the life she'd originally
planned with Jeremy because she couldn't imagine
Adrian being happy with an arrangement that
afforded him anything less than fifty percent of his
son's actual time, care, or lodging.

"May I make a suggestion?" Mr Gray asked.

"Of course."

"Is there any way you two can work out your differences? Seek counseling, perhaps?"

"I…I don't know."

"As I said, I would encourage you to try."

Sabrina left Jonathan Gray's office, completely
uncertain as to what to do next. She didn't want to
give up Jeremy for as much as a single day, but
after seeing how much Adrian loved his son, could
she expect him to willingly do what she couldn't?

What options did she have?

She mulled over Gray's advice for the next few
days until Wednesday evening, when she finally

found the courage to raise the subject with Adrian. After sliding a pan of his favorite brownies into the oven for dessert, she waited for her opportunity.

"I spoke to an attorney the other day," she said offhandedly.

"Oh?"

"He'll draw up a will that appoints you as Jeremy's guardian if anything should happen to me."

For several seconds he didn't answer, as if he was either choosing his words carefully or stopping himself from saying something he might later regret. "I suppose I should admit I did the same."

She was stunned. "You did?"

"Well, my will isn't quite like yours because of the guardianship issue, but if anything happens to me, everything I own will belong to you and Jeremy."

"You did that? For us?"

"Of course." He seemed surprised that she'd asked. "Why wouldn't I?"

"Well..." She hesitated. "What if you meet someone you want to marry?"

"If by some chance I do, wills can always be changed."

Once again, the thought of a stepmother appearing in her son's life didn't sit well in Sabrina's heart. The idea of another woman in *Adrian's* life was equally disconcerting.

"The point is," he continued while she stewed about the possibility, "we have Jeremy's future decided if one of us dies, but what do we do while we're both living?"

She toyed with her fork. "The attorney and I talked about that, too."

He studied her thoughtfully. "And?"

"He suggested we create a parenting plan."

For several seconds, he didn't answer. "Which means what?"

She drew a bracing breath. "We decide if I should have primary physical custody and if we'll share legal custody. That way, we're both involved in any major decisions like Jeremy's education or medical concerns."

"By primary physical custody, you mean he'll live with you three hundred and sixty-five days out of the year."

"More or less."

Once again, he fell silent. "I don't care for your solution."

"I didn't think you would," she said wryly.

"Out of curiosity, what happens if we don't agree on terms?"

"Then the court will decide for us. And..." her breath caught "...most likely, Jeremy will be shuttled back and forth between us." She met his gaze. "I've already made my feelings plain. I don't want Jeremy to be displaced every week."

He rose from the table and scraped his plate into the garbage disposal. "I'm not happy about it either, but what choice do we have?"

What choice, indeed? He already knew the answer by the calm way in which he spoke. He was simply waiting for her to accept and admit it, too.

But could she commit to a wedding because she didn't want to be separated from her son? After all, there was a slight chance the judge would rule in her favor. Adrian's cellphone interrupted her thoughts.

He glanced at the display and smiled. "My sister," he said before he answered.

"Hi, Marcy. I'm in the middle something monumentally earth-shattering and life-changing." His wink in her direction brought a warm glow to her face. "So this had better be good."

His teasing tone disappeared and his smile turned into a worried frown. "Room seven-fifteen. I'll be there. Call me if anything changes." He clicked off the connection.

"What's wrong?"

A cold, hard mask had settled on his face. "It's Clay. He's in hospital."

Her stomach clenched. "Oh, Adrian."

"Apparently he has peritonitis. His so-called food poisoning last week was apparently a leaky appendix. His temperature shot up and he went into a seizure." He jumped up. "I have to go."

"I'll help you pack your bag." After a quick swipe of Jeremy's messy face, she placed him in his playpen and went to the bedroom.

Adrian's suitcase lay open on the bed as he yanked clothes off hangers and tossed them haphazardly in its direction. "I'll do this," she ordered. "Fetch your shaving kit."

He left, presumably for the bathroom, and returned a minute later with his toiletry case in hand.

"Do you want all your clothes or just enough for a day or two?" she asked, poised in front of the closet.

"Enough for a few days. Just casual stuff. If I need anything else, I'll get it from my house."

She quickly folded the clothes meeting his criteria inside the soft-sided case and left the others to hang up later.

As soon as she'd packed his essentials, he zipped the piece of luggage closed and headed for the door.

"You'll drive carefully, won't you?" she asked,

knowing his worry could make him inattentive and impatient behind the wheel.

"Yeah."

"And you'll call me. To tell me how he's doing?"

His "Yeah, sure," sounded so automatic, she wondered if he meant what he'd said. Although if he didn't call, she knew his number.

He paused at the playpen, bent down and kissed Jeremy's cheek, then hurried out of the house.

Sabrina tried not to feel rejected, but she did. Suddenly she was glad they hadn't had the conversation she'd hoped for because his action couldn't have spelled out his feelings any plainer.

She was only a convenience. A means to an end. A necessary evil to live with in order to have access to his son. Granted, he'd been in a hurry when he'd left, but he could have acknowledged her in some way, instead of ignoring her.

Fighting back tears, she began clearing the dishes when suddenly the front door slammed. She turned to see Adrian striding purposely toward her.

"I forgot something," he said.

She blinked the wetness out of her eyes and swallowed the lump in her throat. "I can't imagine what," she said, hating to hear the choked-up sound coming out of her throat.

He planted a hard kiss against her mouth. "I *will* call you," he said, and then he left.

He came back because he'd forgotten to *kiss her*? Oh, my.

She wanted to laugh and cry at the same time. Tears streamed down her face as she sank onto the nearest chair. Adrian's one small action sent her spirits soaring before they crashed with chagrin and embarrassment at how quickly she'd thought the worst, and how badly she'd misjudged his actions.

If they were going to have any sort of future, she had to stop reading events through the veil of her insecurities and have more faith in him. If he was trying to put their past behind him, she couldn't do any less.

The kitchen clean and Jeremy happily entertaining himself, she began straightening the clothes Adrian had discarded in an untidy heap. It didn't take long, but as she retrieved a pair of trousers off the floor, a scrap of paper fell from a pocket. Thinking it might be a phone message or an appointment reminder, she unfolded the slip and saw it was a cashier's check receipt.

Certain he'd need it for business purposes, she laid it on the dresser. Just as she turned away, the amount caught her eye and she froze.

She hadn't misread those numbers. They matched her hospital bill down to the last cent.

Adrian had paid her bill. *Adrian* had been her anonymous benefactor. *Adrian* had wiped out her debt.

How could he do this to her? He *knew* she didn't want his financial support, but he gave it anyway. Accepting the television and the rest of his "surprises" had been difficult enough, but knowing he'd paid her bill was doubly hard to swallow.

What motive did he have?

Righteous anger built. Was he trying to prove she couldn't provide for Jeremy, whereas he could? Or was it strictly conscience money, a way to pay her off and feel good in the process?

Have faith, her conscience whispered.

Shamed by breaking her vow in less than five minutes, she sank weakly onto the bed and scolded herself for jumping to conclusions.

Yes, he was deeply committed to his family and didn't shirk his perceived responsibilities toward them. As Jeremy was now a part of that circle, Adrian probably felt obligated to carry his share of her financial load.

Obligated. Oh, how she hated that word. She didn't want to be anyone's obligation, especially not Adrian's. She wanted him to love her and she desperately wanted to hear those words.

His love for us showed in the things he did and taught us.... He always made time when we needed him.

Why Adrian's description of his father popped into her head at that moment, she didn't know, but now that it had, she judged Adrian's actions by a new standard. Apparently Adrian's father had quietly let his actions speak for himself, which was what Adrian had obviously spent his entire life doing. Carrying the responsibilities of a family was a labor of love, not obligation or duty.

No, Adrian hadn't said he loved her, but she knew he did.

He'd come back to kiss her goodbye.

CHAPTER TEN

ADRIAN sat next to Clay's bed as he watched his brother sleep. IV tubes carried pain meds, fluids, and strong antibiotics while a urinary catheter and an abdominal drainage tube accomplished the opposite.

He paid close attention to the numbers flashing on the monitors. If a problem developed, he intended to catch it in the early stages. At the moment Clay's condition was stable, but he still felt powerless.

Clay would be fine. In his head, he recited those words like a mantra, but he couldn't stop thinking that he shouldn't have accepted his brother's self-diagnosis of food poisoning without asking more questions. He was the doctor in the family, dammit! His family relied on *him* for medical advice.

Some advice he gave. He'd simply told his brother to drink plenty of fluids and lay off the steaks for awhile. He may as well have recommended the famed take-two-aspirin-and-call-me-in-the-morning cure.

Marcy walked in, wearing her favorite hunter-green drawstring trousers and a colorful T-shirt that read, "Teachers have class". A huge bag hung off one shoulder and she balanced a steaming cup of coffee in each hand. "How's he doing?" she whispered.

"Resting comfortably. I see you're still carrying everything but the kitchen sink." He motioned to her purse.

"That's right," she whispered cheerfully as she handed over Adrian's latest dose of caffeine. "Teachers are like Boy Scouts. Our motto is 'Be prepared'. You never know what you'll need or when you'll need it." She nodded in Clay's direction. "What did the doctor say, or is telling me a breach of privacy regulations?"

"Jalil said Clay should be up and around in a few days." Jalil Kedar was Clay's general surgeon as well as Adrian's friend. "He'll be a sick puppy for a while, but they've loaded him with antibiotics so we should see improvement soon."

"Then he won't have any more seizures?"

"His was probably a reaction to his high temperature because he hasn't had any since his temp has come down to near normal. Jalil wants to take a wait-and-see attitude. If it happens again, we'll call in a neurologist."

"Clay's survived his share of medical problems, hasn't he?" she murmured.

"He's definitely met his quota," Adrian said wryly.

Marcy plopped down on a second chair. "It sounds as if he's on the mend, though."

"I think so."

"Then while we're waiting for Clay to finish his nap, I want to hear all about this earth-shattering, life-changing situation you were telling me about." Her eyes sparkled. "Does it have anything to do with a certain woman who's my nephew's mother?"

"You know about Sabrina? And Jeremy?"

She waved a hand. "Of course. Clay couldn't wait to call me with the news after your little dinner the other night. Frankly, bro, I'm disappointed you didn't invite Susan and me."

"It was a last-minute thing."

"So are you and Sabrina back together?" She sounded curious rather than upset or disappointed but, then, she'd told him he'd been a fool a year ago, immediately after he'd broken off their relationship.

"We're still working things out," he replied. "It's complicated."

She sighed. "It always is."

Sabrina waited all evening for Adrian's promised update and when the phone didn't ring, she lifted the receiver several times to verify she had a dial tone. Hating to contact him in case the situation was critical and he couldn't talk, she told herself not to worry.

He finally called her late Thursday morning. "Clay is doing OK. The antibiotics seem to be working, although he isn't too perky yet."

She heard the note of exhaustion in his voice and guessed at the cause. He probably hadn't left Clay's side, which meant he looked as rough as he sounded.

"I'm guessing you aren't too perky yourself," she said. "You stayed all night at the hospital, didn't you?"

"I slept a few hours here in the room."

Having worked at Mercy, she knew the sleeping arrangements available for family members. "In one of those awful recliners, I'll bet."

"Yeah, but I'll be fine."

"Are your sisters with you?"

"They were yesterday, but not today. Marcy has teacher inservices because school starts next week and Susan had an out-of-town audit she couldn't reschedule."

"I could drive down."

"No. It isn't necessary. Everything's under control."

Of course it was. Adrian would demand nothing but perfection and order. Meanwhile, he was probably driving the nurses crazy.

"Honestly, I don't mi—"

"Gotta go. I'll talk to you later." He disconnected before she could finish. Although she hadn't planned anything exciting for their four-day weekend, she hadn't dreamed they'd spend it in separate cities either.

He'd sounded so tired; he was obviously too intent on watching over Clay to take care of himself. Someone had to convince him to see reason and without any other candidates available, the task fell to her.

After several phone calls and two haphazardly packed bags later—one for Jeremy and one for herself—she exchanged her scruffy pair of denim shorts and formula-stained tank top for her favorite multicolored floral sundress. If she was going to barge into Clay's room without an invitation and brave Adrian's wrath for disobeying his wishes, she wanted the bolstering support of knowing she looked her best. A quick brush of her hair, a touch of eye-shadow, and she deemed herself ready.

As an afterthought, she added the matching lime-green sweater because hospital rooms were often chilly, then loaded Jeremy and their bags into her car. Within fifteen minutes the day-care staff at Pinehaven welcomed Jeremy into their fold and she headed southwest to Mercy Memorial.

An hour and a half later she stepped off the seventh floor elevator and onto her former nursing unit. Room seven-fifteen's door was slightly ajar, so she knocked, then waited a few seconds before strolling across the threshold.

Adrian's face registered surprise as his mouth curved into a welcoming smile. Before it stretched too far, though, he turned it into a frown. "Sabrina. What are you doing here?"

"Isn't it obvious? I came to visit," she said softly, aware of Clay sleeping a few feet away. "How's he doing?"

"The same as a few hours ago. You didn't have to come. I told you everything was fine."

"I know you did, but I wanted to see for myself." She eyed his wrinkled shirt, the dark shadow on his face. "I was right. You look as ragged around the edges as Clay does."

He shrugged, seemingly uncaring about his appearance. "Nothing that a little soap and water won't cure."

"Have you gone home?"

"I came straight here as soon as I arrived in town and I haven't left," he confessed. "My bag is still in the car."

"Maybe you should get it. I'm sure the shower in the doctors' lounge is free. You'll feel a lot better if—"

"I appreciate what you're trying to do, Bree, but I'm a big boy and don't need a mother hen telling me what to do."

She didn't allow his mood to bother her. "Testy today, aren't we?"

"Look," he said, more calmly than before. "I don't need company and, as you can see, neither does Clay."

So much for her mission of mercy. "Trying to give you moral support is like trying to force sour-tasting medicine down Jeremy's throat," she said lightly.

His eyes widened. "Speaking of Jeremy, where is he?"

"At day care. Kate will babysit after her shift ends and—"

"You left him over an hour away?" He sounded horrified.

"I couldn't bring him to the hospital for obvious reasons and I certainly couldn't leave him at your house alone either. I don't have a child-care system here."

"Then you shouldn't have come."

"Jeremy is in good hands. I didn't leave him by the side of the road or alone in an empty house, and I never would. You know that."

He fell silent and she watched him clench and unclench his jaw. It was easy to see how Clay's condition weighed heavily on his mind.

"Talk to me, Adrian. What's really bothering you? Is there a complication you aren't telling me?" She whispered her last comment so Clay couldn't overhear.

He raked a hand through his hair. "No complications. He's doing fine."

"Then why are you acting this way? I love you, so we're supposed to handle problems together." She hadn't meant to blurt out her feelings when she'd wanted to share them under the proper ambience, but the best-laid plans....

"There isn't a problem," he insisted.

"Something is eating you up inside. Why won't you tell me?"

"Go home, Sabrina, where…" His tired voice broke. "Just go home."

"Where? Where I belong?" she asked, certain he would have finished with those words if he hadn't stopped himself.

He didn't answer.

As much as she wanted to argue, to remind him that she wanted to help him fight his demons, she'd plainly lost the battle before it had begun. Struggling with her own disappointment, she said, "OK, I'll leave you, then. Before I do, though, why don't you give yourself a break to shower and shave? I know you don't want to leave Clay by himself, so I'll sit with him in the meantime."

He hesitated, and she guessed why.

"Nothing will happen while you're gone," she told him. "I'll watch out for him."

For an instant his hesitation was obvious, but then he shook his head. "I'm staying."

For a long moment, she watched and waited, trying to sound calm when her emotions whirled like a tornado. "Why are you shutting me out, Adrian?"

"I'm not," he denied.

"You are," she insisted.

"Clay's my responsibility, not yours."

"I'm trying to help *you* help Clay. I'm not trying to take your place."

He fell silent.

Wondering how she would break through his hard-headedness, she gave a final argument.

"According to you, your father showed his love by the things he did for his family. You've obviously learned from his example because I've seen you do kind, thoughtful things for the people who mean a lot to you. So I don't understand why you won't allow anyone to support you in the same way."

To her disappointment, he didn't answer. "You're right. There isn't any reason for me to stay. I don't belong here."

He swiped his face tiredly. "You should be with Jeremy."

"Yes, I should be," she snapped. "He appreciates having me around all the time, not just when it's convenient. I'm curious, though. If I'd accepted your proposal, where would my place be today? Here with you, or at home, out of the way?"

She turned on one sandal and made a beeline for the door, but before she could pull it open, his hand held it shut.

"Clay's my brother," he said simply. "I have to be here. You don't."

"You're wrong, Adrian. It isn't about 'have to's.' It's about 'want to's.' Our place is *together*, but if you can't see that, then you deserve to hold your lonely vigil. Just don't expect me to welcome you back with open arms. In fact, don't expect me to welcome you *at all*, and I don't care how many times you're hit by a golf ball!"

Yanking at the handle, she broke his hold, then slipped into the hallway. Luckily, she didn't run into anyone she knew on her way to the elevator. Adrian McReynolds had driven her to tears in front of her colleagues before. He wouldn't do it again.

She punched the "down" button, overwhelmed by the sense of déjà vu. Once again, he'd rejected her, but she'd finally learned her lesson. As much as she'd admired him for his devotion to his family, it was obvious she'd always play second fiddle.

OK, so maybe she was being somewhat selfish, but she liked to think they'd handle family problems—or any problem for that matter—as a team, not as "his" or "hers". He obviously didn't hold the same philosophy but she wouldn't have it any other way.

The elevator arrived, then descended floor by agonizing floor. Chafing at the delay when she'd hoped for a quick exit, she blinked away the tears burning in her eyes. Now wasn't the time to feel the hurt—that would come later and in private. Right now anger propelled her forward and stopped her from falling on the floor and wailing like a two-year-old.

If Adrian wanted to shoulder his burdens by himself from now until eternity, he could do so with her blessing.

Ever since Marcy's phone call, Adrian had been racked by guilt for not recognizing Clay's symptoms. However, that black cloud was nothing compared to what he was feeling now.

"Idiot." Clay's weak voice broke through Adrian's misery. "You're an absolute, certifiable idiot."

Adrian privately agreed.

"You had a good thing and let it slip through your hands again." Clay rubbed his eyes. "For a man who always told us to learn from our mistakes, you don't follow your own advice."

He struggled to raise himself, but Adrian intervened. "What are you doing?"

"Trying to get up so I can punch your lights out," Clay retorted, although his shakiness contradicted his threat.

"Settle down. I got the message." Adrian gently pushed his brother onto his pillows and checked the IV lines to confirm Clay hadn't unseated them. "I assume you heard?"

"Enough to know my supposedly intelligent brother cornered the market on stupidity and insensitivity."

"OK, OK," Adrian said impatiently. "I got your point."

"Why *do* you keep pushing Sabrina away?" Clay's gaze narrowed. "What would have been wrong with letting her sit here while you cleaned up? Frankly, brother, you look worse than I feel."

"Gee, thanks."

"Honestly, I don't know why you think I need you to hold my hand."

"It's what Mom and Dad would have done."

"So you still intend to take their place until we're both gumming our food?" Clay muttered a harsh expletive. "Dammit, Adrian, I didn't ask you to sit beside me when I wrecked my cycle. I didn't ask you to come running now. I appreciate your time and concern, but you don't *have* to be here."

Adrian winced. "You heard that?"

"And a whole lot more. What I'm trying to say is I'll always need my big brother, but not in the way I did when I was eight years old. Your responsibilities have changed. Marcy and Susan and I shouldn't take first place. Sabrina and your son belong there."

For the last twenty-four hours Adrian had been struggling with how to juggle his responsibilities toward his old family with those of his new one, but now, losing Sabrina was more than he could bear.

"You know," Clay said kindly, as if their brotherly hierarchy were reversed, "Dad may have asked you to look after us, but he wouldn't have wanted you to stop living your own life."

Clearly he *had* gotten stuck in his surrogate father role. One thing was certain—if he'd been torn up by their separation before, he wouldn't survive it now.

Only a few minutes had passed; Sabrina couldn't have gotten far. He jumped to his feet and headed toward the hallway. "I have to catch her before she leaves."

"Don't come back unless she's with you," Clay called after him.

Adrian bolted for the elevator, but the display showed it had stopped on the second floor. He couldn't wait for it to meander back to the seventh. He sprinted for the stairs and flew down the twisting and turning steps as if he was running for his life.

Maybe he was.

He had to get to Sabrina before she drove away.

He burst onto the main floor, struggling for breath as he scanned the lobby for her brightly colored dress.

There she was, several feet from the front entrance! He sprinted forward, calling her name.

She paused to listen, but as he yelled her name again, she ignored him and went on.

He skirted several people in his race to intercept her before she reached the door. A heartbeat later, he grabbed her arm. "Sabrina, wait."

She stopped and stared coldly at him. "Let go of my arm or I can guarantee we'll both be on the evening news. You, *Dr McReynolds*, will be a public relations nightmare for Mercy Memorial."

He held on. "Please, wait. I have to talk to you. Explain."

"What's to explain? You don't want me sharing this part of your life, so I won't. I'm going home to *my* son, where *I* belong. By the way, don't worry about your things. They'll be waiting on the front lawn for you when you get back, so you'd better pray it won't rain in the meantime.

"Oh, and my attorney will be in touch with a visitation schedule. I'll warn you it won't be generous."

Adrian moved quickly to stand in front of her. "Don't go. Please."

She gave a most unladylike snort. "Why shouldn't I?"

"Because I love you."

Her eyes suddenly glistened, but she rapidly blinked away the moisture. "No, you don't. If you loved someone, you wouldn't hold a part of yourself back and you wouldn't push the other person away."

"I'm sorry."

"I'm sure you are. Now, either turn me loose or I'll scream."

He held on, his steely-eyed gaze unwavering as he met hers, hoping she'd see what lay in his heart.

Ready to follow through on her threat, Sabrina opened her mouth to draw in a breath, but before her lungs filled to capacity, his mouth covered hers in a hard, bruising kiss.

She resisted at first, then, too emotionally drained to protest, gave up. Attune to her surrender, he gentled himself, kissing her until she began kissing him back. Oh, how she hated her weakness where Adrian McReynolds was concerned.

"Oh, get a room," a blue-haired lady snapped as she walked by. "This is a hospital, not a seedy hotel."

A seedy hotel? The words snapped Sabrina out of her haze and she began to giggle, more as result of her conflicting emotions than from any humor.

"Come on." Adrian pulled her over to a cozy visitors' nook and guided her into an overstuffed chair. After she was settled, he perched on the edge of a solid walnut coffee table.

She wondered if he realized how he'd placed himself at her feet, then decided it didn't matter. "You're wasting your time, Adrian. I don't have the fortitude to go through this time after time. I'm saying enough."

"I want to tell you a story."

Crossing her arms petulantly, she snapped, "I don't want to hear it."

"I want to begin on a day about seventeen years ago," he continued as if she hadn't spoken. "A week before my eighteenth birthday."

She tapped her foot. "This has nothing to do with—"

"Bear with me, Bree. My parents and I had gone to a used-car lot to shop for a car for me. On the way home, I was driving. The driver of a cattle truck ran a red light and hit us. I'd swerved, but I wasn't fast enough. The passenger side of the vehicle was crushed. Mom was killed instantly."

He'd drawn her into his story and she could only gasp and keep listening. "I'm so sorry. You never told me the details."

"It was too painful, so I didn't. And I didn't get more than a few scratches and bruises. Someone called an ambulance and the fire department used the Jaws of Life to cut my dad out of the wreckage. I talked to him the whole time, holding his hand and begging him to hang on.

"He knew he wasn't in good shape. He made me promise to look after my sisters and Clay, no matter what. I did. I would have promised him whatever he'd asked for because I felt responsible. If I hadn't been so eager to buy that car, we wouldn't have been at that intersection. Maybe if my dad had been driving, he could have avoided the crash. Because of all that, I robbed my little brother and younger sisters of their parents."

"You never told me. You should have," she gently accused.

"Probably, but I don't talk about it. It brings up bad memories and old feelings I'd like to forget."

She leaned forward. "But the accident wasn't your fault. You didn't run that stoplight. And who knows if your father could have swerved in time? Maybe if he had, *you* would have been killed. You just don't know and you can't blame yourself for events outside your control."

"Maybe not, but since then I've taken my responsibilities toward my family seriously. When Clay got the idea to buy a motorcycle, he asked me for the money. He'd been scrimping for a long time, but he'd only saved half the amount. Then he found a used cycle advertised in the paper. It was such a good deal, he hated to pass it up. And I hated to see him spend more money for the identical thing, so I gave in and loaned him the balance.

"A few weeks later, he had the accident. Naturally, I felt guilty and was angry at myself for going against my better judgement. I'd failed him once, you see, and I was determined to work with him twenty-four seven if that's what it took to help him walk again. So I broke off things with you."

"And you did it again today," she reminded him. "Don't tell me you're holding yourself responsible for his peritonitis."

"I *am* the doctor in the family. I should have sensed something was seriously wrong with my brother."

"Adrian." She took his hand. "When you were a kid, did you have accidents or illnesses?"

He stared at her. "You have to ask? Of course I did. Who doesn't? I fell out of a tree and gashed my chin. It took ten stitches to close it. I broke my arm one summer playing football and broke off several teeth when I took a header into home plate during baseball season. I also had my tonsils removed because I had frequent sore throats."

"Did your parents feel guilty because you got hurt or because you needed surgery?"

"They didn't act like it." Understanding suddenly dawned in his eyes.

"I think you're trying to fill your parents' shoes and you've lost sight of several facts. One, life happens. We get sick, we need surgery, whatever it might be. Two, Clay and your sisters make their own decisions. They aren't children needing your protection."

He looked sheepish. "That what Clay said, too."

"They're adults and all they need is your love and support, which is all Jeremy and I want, too."

"You'll have it," he promised. "I love you, Bree."

Hearing the words thrilled her and yet they still had a few more issues to iron out. "Are you sure?"

"Absolutely. I lived without you for a year and I can't lose you again."

"Then you can't keep pushing me away, Adrian. Our relationship isn't like golf, where we each play individually. We should function like a football team where we work together. What concerns you concerns me."

He nodded. "I know I've screwed up twice, but can we try this again?"

As she gazed into his face, she knew she owed it to herself and to Jeremy to give him another chance. Yes, they could fail, but somehow she sensed they wouldn't.

"You know what they say." Her voice was filled with emotion. "'Third time's the charm'."

His smile slowly grew. In a flash he rose, pulled her into his arms and kissed her until her toes curled.

Finally, he raised his head. "It will be, Bree. It will be."

EPILOGUE

Two years later

"I REALLY think you should rest in the clubhouse," Adrian said as he eased off the brake and headed the golf cart toward the twelfth hole of the Pinehaven Public Golf Course. "You're nine months pregnant and have absolutely no business riding around the links."

Sabrina rested her hands on her massive tummy and rubbed away another twinge. She'd been having those pains off and on for the last two days but if she'd mentioned them, Adrian would have whisked her to the hospital faster than she could yell "Fore". She wasn't going to be stuck indoors because of Braxton-Hicks' contractions.

"I need the fresh air," she said instead. "Besides, bumping around in a cart might shake Junior loose. He's obviously forgotten he was supposed to arrive last week."

"Junior? It's probably a girl and she's late because she's still primping and preening."

She laughed. "For the record, I do not primp or preen."

"And Jeremy and I don't forget. We may get side-tracked or postpone things, but we don't forget."

"I stand corrected."

"But speaking of getting sidetracked, you're the reason why I'm playing badly today. I'd shoot a better score if I wasn't worrying about you."

"Excuses, excuses," she teased.

He swerved to avoid a pothole in the cart path and she grabbed the armrest to hold on. "Sorry," he said.

Her twinge felt stronger. "You should be," she said. "I think you sent Junior into a somersault."

"I still think you should be lounging in the clubhouse."

"And miss all the action?" She shook her head. "Not a chance. I can sit in the cart just as easily as I can sit in a chair."

"We've seen enough action the last two years," he informed her. "It's always our family who lands in the spotlight. I'm hoping this year's benefit tournament will be different."

Another twinge. "Keep hoping," she muttered under her breath. "Granted, the first year was unplanned excitement when I sliced the ball and beaned you. But it turned out well, I'd say." She smiled at him. "We got back together and Pinehaven Health Center recruited its very own full-time emergency services specialist.

"And you can't complain about last year's events because we planned our wedding in advance," she continued. "No unexpected surprises there." After the final team had completed their eighteen-hole round, Sabrina and Adrian had celebrated their wedding. The ceremony had been a well-kept secret and only a handful of people knew the couple had organized the service to take place after the tournament in the clubhouse where everyone had been invited.

"I don't want to deliver my own baby on a green," he said as he slowed down and parked near the tee box. "I personally think Kate's lottery is going to jinx us and we won't get to the hospital in time."

In light of the prominent role Sabrina and Adrian had played in previous tournaments and to generate interest in this year's event, Kate had started taking bets as to the precise hole where Sabrina would go into labor. Tickets were ten dollars each and all proceeds went into the patient benefit fund.

Winners would have their pictures taken with the community's newest arrival.

"I don't believe in jinxes and, besides, the contest is for a good cause." Another cramp hit and she surreptitiously glanced at her watch. They were closer together than she'd thought.

Adrian drew his driver out of his bag, then joined the rest of his team on the tee box. Sabrina impatiently drummed her fingers on her knee.

By the time he returned to the cart with a smile on his face for his long drive, she held the armrest in a white-knuckled grip. As soon as the contraction eased, she said, "The twelfth hole is someone's lucky number."

He stared at her. "What?"

"We need to head to the hospital."

"I knew it. I knew it." He hit the accelerator pedal and the cart shot forward, careening along the path until he veered onto the course itself in an obvious attempt to take a shortcut.

"You can't cut across," she gasped. "You'll tear up the grass."

"Ask me if I care," he said grimly, gripping the steering-wheel as if he were participating in the Indy 500.

He rolled past a group of golfers who began to

cheer as if they guessed why he was driving like a maniac. "Adrian, you can slow down. We have plenty of time."

He screeched to a halt in front of the clubhouse and a crowd of well-wishers, including Kate, hurried her to his car.

Fifteen minutes after Sabrina arrived at the hospital, Susannah Marie McReynolds made her appearance.

Sabrina watched as Adrian held the swaddled little body in his arms. "She's beautiful," he said.

"She is," Sabrina agreed. He perched on the edge of the bed and held the baby so she could see Susannah's face. "Oh, dear, she has my nose."

"And a gorgeous nose it is," he said, before he leaned over and kissed her. "Thank you for our daughter, my love."

Sabrina smiled tiredly at him. "You're welcome."

"There are a few people waiting outside the nursery to meet their new niece and sister. Do you mind if I show her off?"

Did she mind? Not at all. In fact, hardly anything upset her these days and the same applied to Adrian. Family and friends filled their life and love tied them all together.

MEDICAL™

Large Print

Titles for the next six months…

April

ITALIAN DOCTOR, DREAM PROPOSAL	Margaret McDonagh
WANTED: A FATHER FOR HER TWINS	Emily Forbes
BRIDE ON THE CHILDREN'S WARD	Lucy Clark
MARRIAGE REUNITED: BABY ON THE WAY	Sharon Archer
THE REBEL OF PENHALLY BAY	Caroline Anderson
MARRYING THE PLAYBOY DOCTOR	Laura Iding

May

COUNTRY MIDWIFE, CHRISTMAS BRIDE	Abigail Gordon
GREEK DOCTOR: ONE MAGICAL CHRISTMAS	Meredith Webber
HER BABY OUT OF THE BLUE	Alison Roberts
A DOCTOR, A NURSE: A CHRISTMAS BABY	Amy Andrews
SPANISH DOCTOR, PREGNANT MIDWIFE	Anne Fraser
EXPECTING A CHRISTMAS MIRACLE	Laura Iding

June

SNOWBOUND: MIRACLE MARRIAGE	Sarah Morgan
CHRISTMAS EVE: DOORSTEP DELIVERY	Sarah Morgan
HOT-SHOT DOC, CHRISTMAS BRIDE	Joanna Neil
CHRISTMAS AT RIVERCUT MANOR	Gill Sanderson
FALLING FOR THE PLAYBOY MILLIONAIRE	Kate Hardy
THE SURGEON'S NEW-YEAR WEDDING WISH	Laura Iding

MILLS & BOON®

MEDICAL™

Large Print

July

POSH DOC, SOCIETY WEDDING	Joanna Neil
THE DOCTOR'S REBEL KNIGHT	Melanie Milburne
A MOTHER FOR THE ITALIAN'S TWINS	Margaret McDonagh
THEIR BABY SURPRISE	Jennifer Taylor
NEW BOSS, NEW-YEAR BRIDE	Lucy Clark
GREEK DOCTOR CLAIMS HIS BRIDE	Margaret Barker

August

EMERGENCY: PARENTS NEEDED	Jessica Matthews
A BABY TO CARE FOR	Lucy Clark
PLAYBOY SURGEON, TOP-NOTCH DAD	Janice Lynn
ONE SUMMER IN SANTA FE	Molly Evans
ONE TINY MIRACLE…	Carol Marinelli
MIDWIFE IN A MILLION	Fiona McArthur

September

THE DOCTOR'S LOST-AND-FOUND BRIDE	Kate Hardy
MIRACLE: MARRIAGE REUNITED	Anne Fraser
A MOTHER FOR MATILDA	Amy Andrews
THE BOSS AND NURSE ALBRIGHT	Lynne Marshall
NEW SURGEON AT ASHVALE A&E	Joanna Neil
DESERT KING, DOCTOR DADDY	Meredith Webber

MILLS & BOON®